THE
VINE

Arlene Adamo

Dedicated to all the African ancestors who were stolen from their homes, taken to a foreign land and forced into a life of cruel slavery

Chapter 1

Mary leaned over the edge of the bow, and took in a long deep breath of cold sea air. With no moon in the sky, the ocean seemed dark and endlessly empty. The creaking of the ship sounded like the pitiful whines of a dying old man. Although the waves were low and inconsequential, Mary could feel the hidden might of the water as it gently tossed the vessel. With such power, why did the ocean tolerate this weak creation of man? Why did she not just rise up and crush this thing, that by its very existence, seemed to mock her greatness. Could it be that the ship was not worthy of even a minor effort of destruction, or did she hold back only as an expression of God's endless Mercy and Grace?

Mary had been warned not to come on deck at night in case she was either washed away or snatched by Leviathan himself, but the smell below deck was too much to bear. She also desperately needed to see the star-filled sky to reassure herself that beauty still existed, despite the disparaging circumstances she now faced.

This miserable boat was a long way from her comfortable sweet smelling rooms at home. She yearned for her soft stuffed bed and clean linens. Her memories of laughter, affectionate little dogs, beautiful music and other amusements, were all she had to try and fill her despairing moments. And oh, how much she missed her maid servants—girls with sweet voices and clean smiling faces who would cheerfully attend to her needs.

Her brother Charles had denied her even a single servant on this voyage. *If you believe that you can make choices like a man, than you shall live like one. But, sweet sister, do not imagine that you deserve the life of a nobleman. Your disobedience has earned you only a simple man's life, and that is what you shall receive.*

Not only did he arrange this unbearable journey on such a foul ship, but he deliberately commissioned a cargo vessel with no other female aboard. Although she was protected from physical harm—because all aboard had been warned of her brother's power and what he would do to any man who touched her—she was not safe from their stares on deck or leers through the chinks in the walls of her cabin. She tried to stuff the openings with bits of cloth, but it would not be long before she would find the bits pushed out again and lying on the floor.

The first night she didn't sleep at all for the sound of scurrying rats and mice over the floors and walls. After several nights of barely any rest, she finally succumbed to a deep sleep, and after that was capable of ignoring the scratching noises of the vermin.

The food, although plentiful enough, was hardly tolerable. Between the slop she was given to eat and the constant rocking of the ship, she never ceased to feel a sickly pain in her stomach.

It had been several days since she changed her clothes, and she was now feeling as though the dirt was beginning to seep into her very skin. She could have spent more time trying to keep clean, but surrounded by so much filth, she could see little reason to bother. Also, she wanted to protect herself from the prying eyes in the walls. At home, she bathed morning and evening, and had been used to having servants change her gown two or more times within a single day.

Initially, she was very frustrated with her hair, having always depended on the skills of others to keep it fashionably sculpted. Despite attempts, she could not figure out how to keep it up in even the simplest way. She finally resolved to leave it natural, and just hide it away under a cap or bonnet.

The one thing she dreaded the most was being forced to empty her own chamber pot into the sea. At least twice a day, she had to carry it up from her room past the sailors who would shamelessly stare at her. It was even worse when she was also forced to empty pails of red water left from having to wash out her own bloody rags.

There was one crew member in particular who always seemed to be waiting for her. He was a toothless old gargoyle who would grin as he watched her throw the contents of her pot overboard. One time, just as she had emptied it, a wind suddenly picked up sending the urine back and down the front of her dress. The delighted gargoyle bellowed in disgusting laughter. Although she tried as best she could to avoid this repulsive creature, he would always be there, lying in wait.

Mary looked out at the darkness of the ocean. She had no idea where the ship was taking her, but only knew that it was taking her farther and farther away from England. When would this nightmare end? Tears ran down her cheeks and she whispered into the wind, "*My God, why hast Thou forsaken me?*"

"She has said what?" The Duke of Compton shouted, lurching forward from his gilded chair, and slamming his open hands down on the long dark polished table in front of him. His face had turned beat red in anger.

"Your Grace," said the frightened man, eyes firmly fixed on the floor, "she said she would never marry Lord William."

"Damn that woman!" the Duke muttered through his firmly clenched jaw. "What makes her believe that she has any say in the matter? It is I who will tell her where she shall go, what she shall do and whom she shall marry. All my life she has questioned my authority, and now she dares to say that she will not marry the one man who I have deemed the right match. I have the Divine right to make this decision, not her. God, Himself, gives me that right!"

The Duke knew that she would not be happy about his order for her to marry—and especially if the groom was to be William—but he never dreamed she would be so defiant as to refuse the order outright. Perhaps there would be some female sulking, a few tears and even a small inconvenient sabotage of the wedding plans, but never blatant defiance.

"The foolish woman must be made to know her place. Go back and tell her, if she will not marry her cousin, then she is as good as dead. I have more than one sister, but she has only one life," said the Duke, determined that his sister was not going to win this battle.

The man, still never once looking up, mumbled, "Yes Your Grace," and then slowly backed out of the room.

"Your Grace," said a voice from the shadows.

The Duke knew from his tone what was coming, and felt annoyed whenever his advisor Edmund lectured him. In fact, the man so annoyed him that he would not have hesitated to have him killed outright. However, the advice Edmund provided, although unwanted, was always sound and proved vital in increasing both the Duke's fortune and his power.

"Yes, yes, I know," said the Duke, sitting back in his chair and waving his hand like he was waving away a fly. "She is of The Vine, and must be protected under any circumstances. I know my duty Edmund, and I would never go against the law of The Family. I would never harm her. Still, I am tired of her insubordination. She must be taught a lesson that she will never forget. You know that she has been like this even as a child. Ever since she could talk, she has shown no regard for me. It is my duty to make her understand that her life is not her own. Her life is in my hands to guide as God instructs me. Mary has always been a hysterical woman without the benefit of a man's reason, and difficult as it may be for me, my responsibility is to tame her as one would any wild animal."

"Your Grace," said Edmund, bowing respectfully, "just please, when deciding how you will tame her, do not forget who she is, and what she means to you."

The Duke felt angry that a man of far lesser birth would dare suggest that he didn't know what he was doing. Still, he had to keep his temper in check when it came to Edmund. This was one underling he could not afford to lose.

"Oh dear simple Edmund, you of all people know that all of my decisions are right and perfect as they come straight from God. Mary is of no value if she is maimed or dead. I will ensure that she remains alive and healthy. But I am afraid that her chance at the honour of marrying Lord William is over and done with. Instead, start arrangements for our younger sister Ann to marry William. I did not plan to see her married until at least her seventeenth birthday, but I have already promised our good cousin William a bride from our mother's line within the year. I should think he would prefer Ann to Mary anyway, as she is far more docile and would make a good and obedient wife."

Substituting Ann for Mary was something that the Duke had not considered until the moment he had uttered those words. He was immensely pleased with himself. This was proving to be yet another wondrous occasion upon which he, as God's chosen, had received holy enlightenment.

"And Mary?" asked Edmund, who was still worried about what sort of lesson the Duke was planning.

"As for my other sister, she will regret the day she ever defied me. Oh, do not worry Edmund. I know my obligation to God. Her life is to be protected at all costs. I promise that I will shed no blood. However, I tell you now that she will learn her place through honest suffering. When I cast her *into the pit that is in the wilderness*, she will beg me for my mercy." The Duke leaned back in his chair and smiled in satisfaction, *for it is written, vengeance is mine!*

Chapter 2

Mary had her eyes firmly fixed on the land which was now clearly visible. When the man from the crow's nest first announced the sighting, she immediately went below and latched the door to her small cabin where she washed and changed into clean clothing. She did not worry about who may be leering through the walls, but only thought about being finally free from this filthy prison. Now, she waited anxiously.

As she stared at the thick forest ahead, she wondered why there were no people or buildings in sight. As far as the eye could see, there were only trees. She had expected to see a bustling port out in the open like those in England, but there was no port visible. There was only a wide river flanked by thick and seemingly impenetrable vegetation.

A tall merchant ship suddenly appeared at the river's mouth, and moved out into the sea. Several other ships followed after. Somewhere hidden along that river was the port where she knew she would be disembarking. Not being able to see any signs of human life, left her feeling fearful of what may still lie ahead. Perhaps the verminous ship that brought her here was not the worst part of her exile.

The ship moved slowly up the river. After what seemed like a very long time, the port finally came into view. Mary was surprised that such a large and busy port would be so deeply hidden inland. There were many people teaming about, and several large ships were docked there including warships. She saw a number of different flags flying on the masts, but the flag of France was the only one she recognized.

As the old vessel pulled up to the pier, Mary could see that many of the men loading cargo onto the other ships were Africans. She had seen pictures of these people in books, but never any in real life. Most of what she knew of the world was only from books, as her brother was very strict about where she could travel, and with whom she could associate.

The whisky-weathered Captain slouched towards her. He only ever spoke to Mary when it was absolutely necessary. She knew that her brother had been very precise in his orders as to how and when she should be addressed. "Me Lady," he said in a loud and disdainful voice, "he waits for you." His dirty hand pointed towards the plank.

The Captain was relieved to know that she would be finally getting off of his ship. He deeply resented her presence. She was a burdensome cargo that distracted his crew who were not easy to control at the best of times. Because of her, he was forced to use the lash far more frequently, and at one point had to throw a man completely overboard.

Mary anxiously walked over to the gang board, and was looking down to find a safe place to set her foot when a gentle and cultured man's voice said, "My Lady, please allow me." She looked up, and was startled to see a very handsome and impeccably dressed man with piercing slate blue eyes holding out his hand to her. His dark blond hair was neatly pulled back under his three cornered hat. Mary was immediately pleased to see that he did not wear a wig. She had always found wigs ridiculous things even for herself.

After spending so long on the old ship and seeing only the roughest and basest of men, this was like a drink in the desert. To have a handsome well-dressed man before her seemed like a wonderful dream, and it made her legs go a little weak. Mary was unsure if she would be able to keep from crumbling in grateful relief for the offer of this gentleman's hand.

With a thankful smile, she silently placed her hand in his. Immediately she felt embarrassed that her hand was not soft as it should be, but instead a little rough and dry from the hardships she had endured on the ship. However, the gentleman did not seem to notice at all, and held on firmly as he helped her down the plank. When they reached the dock, he turned to face her. Smiling a genteel smile, he removed his hat, gracefully bowed and said, "Lady Mary, let me introduce myself. My name is Samuel Montford, and I would like to welcome you to America."

+ + +

The meeting had been called for 6:30 pm, but Captain Robert Springsteen, as always, was late. The men, however, did not mind as there was plenty of brandy to drink and tobacco for their pipes. They sat on the over-stuffed French furniture in Samuel Montford's parlor and talked about the Revolution and local gossip.

Montford had called them together in the name of the Brotherhood, but had not yet told them the reason why. They were one of thirteen Center Circles, and ranked high among those thirteen in both influence and power. Whenever Samuel Montford suddenly called a meeting like this, they knew that what he had to tell them must be of extreme importance.

Finally, the parlor door opened and Captain Robert Springsteen, dressed in his hunting clothes, entered with a great bellowing, "Good evening Brothers!"

"Well finally," said James Pierce, annoyed at how the Captain so boldly entered the room. He had never liked nor trusted Springsteen. For most men, he could determine their weaknesses and know how to handle them, but with a man like Springsteen, it was difficult to know where you stood.

"Good Brothers," smiled Springsteen, slapping Pierce on the back, "I hope you did not start the meeting without me."

Pierce sneered at Springsteen. "You know damn well we cannot begin until all twelve of us are present."

Springsteen responded with only a silent smile which he knew would aggravate Pierce the most.

"Brothers," Montford interjected, "we have business to discuss, so let us get right to it. I have been contacted by The Duke of Compton on a very important matter. It is a matter of the highest order."

At the mention of the Duke, even Springsteen became completely attentive. Montford continued, "In about one week's time a ship will arrive in port carrying extremely valuable cargo. The Duke has sent us this cargo for safekeeping. It is not clear for how long we will have this responsibility, only that there is a sacred task being required of us."

"What kind of cargo?" asked Springsteen, who was rarely patient with the secretive and ceremonious ways of the Brotherhood.

Montford looked Springsteen directly in the eye and said, "It is—or perhaps I should say, she is a woman of The Vine." There was a powerful silence in the room.

"But Brother Montford," stammered Pierce, "why here? Why now? What about the war? Does he not realize there is still a war going on?"

Springsteen laughed. "Does he not realize?" he asked sarcastically. "Why, who will benefit more from the Revolution?"

"Brother Springsteen!" shouted Montford, who was always afraid that one day Springsteen's cynicism could get them all killed. He was not happy to admit such men to the higher ranks of the Brotherhood, but Springsteen proved to be of great value to them in their dealings with the Natives.

"The Duke of Compton has given the orders, and we do not question them," said Montford sternly. "He sends us his own sister for safe keeping and we shall keep her safe."

"Where will she stay?" asked Pierce, hoping that, as a married man with the largest plantation and grandest house, his home would be the chosen place.

15

"Well gentlemen," Montford said with a sigh, "this is a very complicated matter. While she is here in America, the lady is to live a life of solitude in exile."

"Exile?" several men said at once. None of them could believe their ears. They had always been taught the importance of The Vine women, and how they are treasures that must be protected at all costs.

"Yes, she is to live in exile," said Montford. "Unfortunately, she has disobeyed her brother, and now she is to live in isolation so that she may come to understand the seriousness of her actions. The Duke has ordered that we are to find her a place to live which is out of the way and solitary. He has given several stipulations regarding her exile. These include that at no time is she to have women around her—no serving women and definitely no female visitors. As well, her comforts should be few. The Duke's own words were 'the basic comforts of a simple man.' He has sent a list of the few things that she is to receive for her daily living, and she will also be allowed only one or two male servants to ensure her survival."

"But is this not against the code of the Brotherhood?" Springsteen asked in amazement. "Our lives are committed to protecting and nurturing The Vine, not slicing away at it."

"Brother Springsteen, this does not sit entirely well with me either," said Montford. "However, the Duke says that it is for her own good, and we must accept that he has her best interest at heart. We are still required to ensure her welfare and protect her life. That has not changed."

Springsteen did not accept that this was entirely in accordance with their oath, but he knew the Duke's power, and that they had no choice but to obey.

Pierce was feeling personally slighted by the exile. The idea that a woman of The Vine would come to America and not stay at his beautiful house was almost too much for his ego to bear. He had worked hard to ensure his movement upward within society, and then within the Brotherhood. "And how can we guarantee this woman's survival with such restrictions?" he complained. "We are at war. All of the best men are still away.

Who is there that can help and protect her? Where would we find even a single male servant who could be trusted to be alone with her? We are bound to protect The Vine at the cost of even our own lives. How can we obey the Duke's wishes, and fulfill our oath to God also?"

Montford ran his hand over his perfectly pulled back hair and then in a sober tone replied, "We have our orders and must obey them. The Duke receives divine inspiration. He is the Chosen One, so his orders come directly from God."

Springsteen silently scoffed at what he had just heard. He wondered if Montford really believed the nonsense he was saying, or was he merely trying to justify his own participation in this questionable affair?

"Let us focus on the challenge at hand," said Montford. "We require at least one servant who is exceptionally well trained, and never neglects his work. He must be very discreet and respectful of his master. As well, he must be obedient and docile, yet at the same time have the capacity to fight if the woman needs to be defended. After all, she will be required to live in the wilderness, and a dangerous situation could possibly arise."

Springsteen laughed and said, "A man who is as docile as a rabbit, but as powerful as a bear?"

"Well, yes" said Montford, "and on top of that, we need to find a servant who knows his place, and would not be tempted by being alone with a woman."

Springsteen laughed even louder, and the other men in the room joined in. Montford, the one who would eventually have to answer to the Duke, was not as amused. He tried to bring the meeting back on track and said, "There are men who are perhaps more docile—more like women. If we could find the right one, following the rest of the Duke's orders would be easy."

"It sounds as though we require something that is half a man," said Springsteen, who was enjoying the new jovial atmosphere of the meeting.

"Where do you find a half a man?" asked Pierce, who couldn't resist getting in on the joke.

"Try England," shouted out one of the others, and all of the men burst into laughter. Even Montford broke out into a smile. The men had never questioned the paradox of their loyalty to the Duke, yet their view of England as their enemy. These were considered two separate issues.

"Brothers, we must be serious now," said Montford, determined to bring the meeting to order. "We must find a capable servant who would not be a threat to any woman. If only we still had eunuchs." As Montford absently spoke these words aloud, he realized how foolish they were, and how they were also a sign of his growing desperation.

"A eunuch?" laughed Springsteen. "I guess we could always make one ourselves. What about the old merchant Anderson?" Again, the men burst out laughing as each of them knew what it was like to do business with the cunning Mr. Anderson.

Montford did not smile this time, but instead sighed in frustration. He wished that he could make this problem go away. There were so many important matters to be considered with the war almost over, and this was just complicating everything. How could they possibly find a suitable servant when just finding decent help of any sort was so difficult? Still, he was determined that he would fulfill the Duke's orders just the same as he had always done.

"Brothers," he said, "I have already determined a place where she will stay. It is the old home of the dead Tory, Josiah Walker, just north of your land Brother Pierce. The simple log cabin is still in good shape, and could be repaired. There is a small barn to shelter a cow and several chickens. It also has an additional shack that could be made suitable for one or two servants. The small outbuildings that are still standing can be used for storage. I am certain that such a place would be agreeable to the Duke, and should require only a little work to make it suitable. It is far enough out of the way that she should be kept from all people, but it is close enough that I may easily visit with her every three weeks as I have been instructed."

When he first heard that the woman would be staying only several miles from his own home, Pierce was elated, but now hearing that Montford had been given the privilege of contact with her, his happiness changed to resentment. Pierce increasingly felt that he deserved the role that Montford now played within the Center Circle. Montford after all had been unsuccessful in many of his business dealings, and if not for his family contacts and English education, he would be as ordinary as any dirt farmer.

Pierce, on the other hand, was a true conqueror who could eventually be compared to any king or emperor in history. Surely, he was the one who had the God-given right to be close to a woman of The Vine.

Montford, in trying to encourage the men to come up with some helpful ideas, decided that now was a good time to mention the payment. He waited for a moment of silence, to ensure he had everyone's full attention, and then said, "As for finding servants, or even one suitable servant, there is a great deal of money to be made by the servant himself, plus a very generous purse to the fellow who finds him."

Montford looked at each man hoping that the offer of money would entice a possible solution. He added, "I realize that the Revolution has made this task far more difficult. However, any prospect, no matter how uncustomary, is welcome to be heard."

Springsteen, who had been listening intently, began to grin. The thought of making a large sum of money very quickly was extremely appealing. As the last several years had been devoted to fighting the war, there had been almost no opportunity for him to grow his own fortune. He had also heard rumors that made him wonder if he would be sufficiently compensated for his sacrifice once the war was officially over. These concerns prompted Springsteen to come up with an idea that could possibly earn him all of the money being offered. He just had to convince the other men that the idea was sound. Still smiling, he asked, "You say there is a great deal of money to be made by both the servant and the man who finds him?"

"That is correct Brother Springsteen. Do you have an answer to our problem?" Montford asked hopefully.

"I may just have the perfect solution," said the Captain.

"Please Brother Springsteen," said Montford enthusiastically, "share with us what you are thinking."

Springsteen thought for a moment, and then said "First, I would like to ask an earnest question. What if this servant happens to be the slave of the man who finds him? Does the finder then receive both the finder's fee and the servant's wages?"

"A blackie!" shouted Pierce in outrage. "You would send a blackie to be alone with this noble lady? The Vine? Will she not suffer enough? How dare you even make such a suggestion! The thought is completely appalling!"

The men at first could not believe that Springsteen would seriously put forth such an idea, but the look on his face told them this was no joke.

"Brother Springsteen, are you mad?" asked Montford. "This gentle woman will be completely on her own with the closest white person being miles away." Montford was confused as he knew Springsteen to be much more of a thinking man than this.

"Brothers, listen to me," said Springsteen, intent on convincing them that what he offered was a viable option. "I have the perfect servant. He is everything that Brother Montford has mentioned plus more. He is strong, a good hunter, capable of growing crops and taking care of livestock, loyal to his master, and on top of that, has all the skills of the finest house slave. And best of all gentlemen, he has no interest whatsoever in women. You all know him well, and by now you must know I am talking about my own personal slave Jupiter."

Captain Springsteen was feeling very pleased that this opportunity had come his way. He had just received orders to return to the north, and he did not want to risk taking his valet with him. So many slaves had already been coerced to the

British side, and he did not want to take the chance of losing his prize man. Now that he could lease him out, and at such a rate as he knew the Duke would pay, was wonderful luck indeed.

Montford knew that everything Springsteen had said about Jupiter was the truth. This slave was certainly the envy of every gentleman around, and a real trophy for Springsteen. He began to seriously consider the idea. "It is true," he said, "that Jupiter has been offered women and has never taken one. Every attempt to have him mated has been unsuccessful." He snickered and added, "Why Brother Springsteen and I even put him in a room alone with a woman for three days and still nothing."

Pierce was feeling envious that Springsteen might reap the rewards being offered. He tried to think of an alternative, but came up with nothing. In a desperate bid to cast doubt on the suggestion, he said, "Brothers, those women were blackies, but this is a white woman. Would he be so docile if he were left alone with her?"

"Brothers," said Springsteen, annoyed that Pierce was going to be difficult, "do you know of any capable man who when given the opportunity with a woman of any color would turn down such a chance?"

All of the men were silent, including Pierce.

Springsteen continued to sell his idea and said, "Nowhere else would we be able to find such a perfect match for the job. Please think about it. Jupiter has been with me for twelve years now, and never has there been any hint of disobedience. This Negro knows his place. He is of the highest caliber of gentleman's slave. Every one of you knows what he is like. Many of you have leased him out for various functions. Even you, Brother George, have offered me an extraordinary price for him. If you had any worries at all, would you be willing to bring him into your home where your wife and daughters sleep? Jupiter is an example of perfect Negro breeding. It is just too bad he will not breed more of them."

The men chuckled again.

Montford scratched his chin in contemplation. "Well, it is true that I have known Jupiter almost as long as I have known

Brother Springsteen, and that he has never been anything but a loyal slave to his master. It is also true that in all those years he has never shown an interest in any female. If we had an alternative white man, I would say that we must hire him, but other than Jupiter, what choice do we have?"

Montford was actually feeling more confident in Jupiter's abilities than those of any white servant he had ever known, although he would never say such a thing out loud.

"Let us take it to a vote," said Montford, eager to have the matter done with. "All those in favor of leasing Brother Springsteen's slave Jupiter, raise your hand."

Every man raised his hand except for Pierce who still held out hope that there might be a way to have the woman stay at his home.

"It is settled then," said Montford, "The Negro, Jupiter, will serve The Vine for as long as the Duke decides her exile should continue. Brother Springsteen will receive both the payment for finding a suitable man as well as the wages that would have been paid to a free man."

Reminding the men of their sworn duty to silence, Montford added, "As you all know, the presence of The Vine is to be treated with the utmost secrecy. No one outside of this Center Circle is to know anything about her. A loose tongue will mean nothing less than death to the man who cannot control it."

The room was completely silent. They all knew that this was no idle threat.

"Brothers," said Montford, "we will now adjourn as I have many arrangements to make on behalf of The Vine. Brother Springsteen, I expect that you will bring Jupiter here tomorrow so that I might explain to him myself what his responsibilities will be. It is imperative that nothing goes wrong."

"Yes sir," said Springsteen who grinned widely and clapped his hands together. It was a pleasant surprise that today such good fortune had landed right in his lap.

Pierce leaned over to Springsteen and whispered, "I will be keeping an eye on your prize blackie, and if anything goes awry, you will both pay dearly."

Chapter 3

There were grey velvet curtains covering all of the windows, so Mary could not see out, and no one could possibly see in. At the dock, Samuel Montford had hurried her inside the waiting coach, and now sat silently opposite her as they rode along. The curtain nearest him was opened just enough to allow some light inside the carriage, but Mary could not see anything from where she sat. She wished that she could throw open all of the curtains and let the light flood in. She wanted to be able to see everything there was to see, but knew that it would be foolish to even try.

In the quiet dimness, Mary felt some relief to finally know that she had been transported to America. It had been very frightening to be sent out, and told nothing of the destination. Now, she could at least imagine a map, and see where she was in relation to her home in England.

She tried to remember all of the things she had read about America. Much of it had to do with murderous Natives. She did not worry, however, because she felt certain that there was more imagination than truth behind the tales. She also believed that it was likely she had known more violent savages in the courts of England, than she would ever meet in America.

On occasion, Mary heard firsthand accounts from people who traveled to the colonies. Mostly, they would just warn her that it was a vile place with few comforts, and absolutely no culture. She understood why her brother would believe that sending her here would be an unmerciful punishment.

Mary looked over at Mr. Montford who respectfully waited for her to initiate a conversation. "Mr. Montford, would you be able to tell me where exactly I am, and where I am going?" she asked, knowing that she would likely not learn much as her brother would surely have given orders that she be told as little as possible.

Montford hoped that she would not ask too many difficult questions. He wanted their meeting to be as pleasant as possible. Reluctantly he replied, "My Lady, I am only allowed to tell you that you are in America, and that your brother has made—well—reasonable provisions for you. You will be provided with adequate food and shelter as well as protection, but I am afraid you will not live in the style to which you are accustomed. Furthermore, your brother has ordered that you are to be isolated with very limited social intercourse. You are to live in the wilderness with only a single servant who will provide some help, although your brother has ordered that certain everyday chores are to be yours alone. Every three weeks, I am required to visit with you and bring supplies, but that is the only social contact you are allowed."

Montford looked into her eyes thinking how lovely they were and added, "I am so very sorry that I cannot do more to serve you, but I am required to obey the wishes of your brother the Duke."

Mary could see that the man was not comfortable about his participation in her exile. She knew how expansive her brother's powers were, and couldn't help feeling a little sorry for Samuel Montford. At that moment, she was just grateful for small mercies and felt obliged to ease his guilt. She smiled at him and said, "Well Mr. Montford, if you are to be my only social contact, then my exile should not be too much of a discomfort."

Montford smiled and blushed. He was well aware that his handsome face and genteel manners had always been attractive to women. Yet, could he be so lucky to have attracted the eye of a woman of The Vine? He had been widowed now for two years, and since learning of Mary's arrival, had found himself daydreaming of romantic possibilities. At the same time, he was well aware that his mother had been connected to The Vine only through associates, and that his actual bloodline, although noble, was not a part of The Holy Family. The Duke would likely never permit such a union, as he believed and followed in the old law that stated The Vine must never split off from itself. However, Montford knew there had been many points in history where exceptions were made. Still, he had to admit to himself that there was not much hope the Duke would ever allow this. Montford would have to be satisfied with his private fantasies, which now would be even more enjoyable after seeing her face and touching her hand.

Mary put her head back, and closed her eyes. Just to be sitting in a padded coach with a clean and proper gentleman was enough for the moment. She did not want to think about where she was going, but only wished to indulge in the small comforts at hand, even if such comforts might only be short-lived.

The coach began to slow, and then stopped. Mary felt as though she had been traveling a very long way, but could not be sure. In her exhaustion, she had fallen asleep earlier in the journey, and had no idea how long she had slumbered. Now completely awake, she was eager to see the place where she was to live.

The carriage door opened, and Montford got out. He then turned, and offered his hand to Mary. As she placed her hand in his and stepped out, she found herself staring at a small dreary log home. She remembered seeing a drawing of a similar dwelling in one of her books. In the picture, the building looked humbly quaint as it was surrounded by flower gardens and happy children; but this did not look like the picture in the book. This was an ugly hovel.

The cabin had a large slightly crooked front porch and a grey weathered door. There was a plain four paned window on one side—the only window. The patchy roof had obviously been repaired recently which gave the whole thing a less than reliable appearance. The only part of the shanty which looked even mildly reassuring was the solid stone fireplace chimney that rose up from the barren ground.

"This, Lady Mary, will be your cottage," said Montford, choosing his words carefully.

For a few seconds, Mary could not say anything. She just stared at the dark grey hovel before her. How long would she be forced to live here? Back home in England, the stables were more luxurious than this.

"Pardon me My Lady," said a strange man's voice.

Mary looked to her left and was surprised to see two smartly dressed gentlemen. Being so overwhelmed at the sight of the miserable little cabin, she had not noticed them standing there. They both stood with their three cornered hats in hand looking curiously at her. The taller of the two had dark features, and had a rough look about him. Although dressed in a formal coat and vest, the clothing could not disguise his lack of refinement. The other was very fair with a thicker body. He had the look of an English gentleman, and wore a very new looking powdered wig. It was this man who had addressed Mary.

"Lady Mary," said Montford, who was not happy that both Springsteen and Pierce had insisted on being there that day, "may I introduce to you Mr. James Pierce and Captain Robert Springsteen." Mary noted that Mr. Pierce was the wig man and Captain Springsteen was the darker one.

Both men smiled, and bowed with the introduction.

Intent on making a good first impression, Pierce quickly said, "My Lady, welcome to America. I would just like you to know that my thirteen hundred acre plantation is just south of here. It is only a little over an hour's ride at a good gallop. If there is anything I can do for you, within of course the limitations set by your esteemed brother The Duke of Compton, please do not hesitate to ask." Pierce grinned with his teeth and grandly swept his hat onto his head.

"Lady Mary," said Springsteen, who was amused by Pierce's attempt at airs and graces, "I, too, am at your service as it is allowed." In a motion that undoubtedly mimicked Pierce, he also swept his hat up onto his head. He then looked at Pierce who returned the look with an annoyed sneer. How dare Springsteen mock him in front of the woman!

Mary pretended to ignore the obvious animosity between the two men and said, "It is indeed a pleasure to make the acquaintance of such kind and noble gentlemen, as *I am a stranger in a strange land*."

"Lady Mary," said Montford, closing the coach door to reveal the man behind it, "this is your slave Jupiter who will both assist and obey you."

Mary had previously not thought about who could have opened the coach door. She was now surprised and intrigued to finally come face to face with a real African. He did not look at all like the comical drawings in her books. His face had a very serious look to it, like a fastidious student. He appeared to be around six feet in height which made him the tallest among the men there. Also, he was impeccably dressed in a full suit which included a bright white cravat, white stockings below his black breeches and black shoes with shining silver buckles. In his hands he held a three pointed hat. His eyes never left the ground, and he silently bowed in an obedient fashion.

"Good day Mr. Jupiter," said Mary, as she would have addressed any servant.

"Oh My Lady, no!" said Pierce, a little too sharply. Immediately realizing he had overstepped the bounds, he bowed and lowered his tone, "I beg your pardon My Lady, but this is a blackie slave. He is here to obey orders, and only that. His name is Jupiter, and only Jupiter. You must never address him as mister."

Montford did not like how Pierce had felt so at liberty to speak to Mary. It was, however, a benefit that, next to an uncouth clod such as Pierce, he would stand out as a proper and refined gentleman. With a calm and smooth voice he said, "Lady Mary, what Mr. Pierce means to say is that there are no formalities when it comes to slaves. You need only give orders."

"Also, you must give discipline where need be," interjected Pierce. "It is important to be firm with slaves. They are not at all like us you know. You would no more address him as Mr. Jupiter than you would address your horse as Mr. Horse." Pierce chuckled slightly, but stopped when no one else joined in.

Montford felt that he should provide a more delicate clarification and said, "Lady Mary, I realize that you have not been well acquainted with slavery. Slaves are like servants in that they do all the things that our servants would do. The difference is that they are Negroes which make them intellectually inferior. They are not quite animals, but in between mankind and animals. Unlike us, they do not have souls. God placed them on this earth to serve, and that is their only purpose. Jupiter is a particularly excellent example of this specimen being wholly trustworthy and obedient. Be assured that we have provided you with only the best."

Mary looked at Jupiter who continued only to look at the ground. She was not unfamiliar with the ideas that Mr. Montford had just explained to her. In fact, she personally knew the man who wrote the book. He was a physician who first became well-respected among England's elite for his new and modern techniques in bleeding. When there appeared to be an increase in anti-slavery sentiment, this physician was commissioned by slave traders to write a book which he entitled, "A Full Descriptive Report on The Nature of the Negro." Although many in England took it seriously because of the physician's reputation, Mary understood that the book was a fabrication meant to ensure the continuation of slavery. She knew that she must eventually explain this to Mr. Montford, but for now, she said nothing.

"Lady Mary, even though Jupiter may look frightening to you," said Springsteen, whose experience taught him that all women of upper society were neurotically skittish and over-reactive, "he is completely harmless. For over twelve years, he has been my own personal slave, and has always shown himself to be obedient and docile. Please be assured that we are completely devoted to The Vine, and would do nothing to put your welfare in jeopardy."

Pierce added, "And if ever he was to get out of hand, even in the smallest way, my plantation is not far, and I would be here quickly to deal with him."

Mary looked at Pierce's grinning face. The slave did not frighten her, but there was something about Pierce that did.

"My Lady, we must leave fairly soon," said Montford. "So if you please, I will show you the cottage, and provide you with a tour of the grounds."

Mary smiled at Montford's choice of words. She could see it was a hovel and the 'grounds' were really only a barnyard. Nonetheless, she was still finding the man charming, and was happy to spend a little time with him before he was to go. "Thank you Mr. Montford," she said warmly, "I have no idea how long my brother will keep me here, but I assume that I should fully prepare myself, and learn all that I must learn."

Chapter 4

The first morning in her new home, Mary could not force herself to get out of bed. It was still spring, and the air was a little cold and crisp. The bed, although not as comfortable as her bed back in England, was more than sufficient. Montford had furnished the place with the best stuffed mattress he could find, along with some excellent quality linens.

The cabin consisted of only one room. Her large bed was pushed up against the wall, and filled one of the far corners. Beside it was a washstand with a mirror, a basin and a jug. From the bed, she could see the window and fireplace on the opposite wall. Near the window, there were four padded armchairs surrounding a new and polished square table. In the corner at the bottom of her bed was a wardrobe with two large stars carved into the two doors.

Mary realized that Mr. Montford had provided her with comforts that her brother would not have approved, and was feeling very grateful that he took this risk for her. Unfortunately though, the new and elegant furniture seemed only to emphasize the sad and impoverished interior of the cabin.

She looked over at the table, and the single book that rested there. Mr. Montford had explained the day before that she would be allowed only the Bible, and nothing else, to read. Mary knew that Charles had done this to mock her. It was an important part of her life to be able to read every day. At home, she had a large collection of books on every topic imaginable.

To have this taken from her was a hardship, and Charles knew that. He never approved of her interest in the written word, and often complained that it was the books that had poisoned her mind against him.

Mary looked around the room and sadly sighed. At least on the ship, she knew that it would eventually dock, and she would be able to debark. But now, here alone in this hovel, she had no idea when or even if she would ever be allowed to return to her home in England. Mary pulled the covers up tight and began to cry.

Outside the cabin door, Jupiter hesitated. He had an armload of wood and a lantern for making a fire. He hated being given the job of taking care of this woman, and even went so far as to ask his master not to hire him out. Prior to this, he had never asked for anything before.

He was disappointed when his one request ever was absolutely denied. Springsteen told him that the contract had been signed, and there was no backing out. Jupiter never saw the contract, but suspected that the Captain was to make a great deal of money from hiring him out for this job.

He knew about the strange meetings that went on at Mr. Montford's home, and felt that this woman was somehow connected. Jupiter had been told that her presence was to be a complete secret, and that she was very important and must be treated as such. He could not understand, however, why the woman was expected to do certain jobs such as her own laundry. It made no sense that he was to treat her as someone of great importance, and yet only provide limited care. He could only assume that this was because she was there, not only to be hidden, but also to be punished. The entire thing was obviously very complicated, which left him in a very awkward position. It was essential that he approach every moment with extreme caution.

Jupiter was accustomed to dealing exclusively with men, whose reactions he could predict with great accuracy. He had developed a fine skill for understanding the thoughts and expectations of men's minds; and enjoyed a relatively peaceful and uneventful existence because of this. But, what would be the result if he knocked on this door? When he entered the cabin of this foreign woman, who he knew was not accustomed to slaves, how would she react? Would she run terrified and screaming into the woods? Surely such a situation could not possibly end well.

A flock of geese passed noisily overhead. Their loud cacophonous honking awakened Jupiter and somehow gave him the courage he needed to knock on the door.

Mary heard the harsh sound of the geese pass overhead, and then fade quickly into the distance. Their noisy departure left behind a heavy silence in the cabin. She began to think about getting out of bed, when she heard a soft knock on the door. Slowly placing her feet on the cold rough floor, she stood up, and wrapped herself in the down filled cover. Cautiously she walked to the door, where she stopped to listen again. Mary was now unsure if the knock was real, or if she had just imagined it. With the only world she had ever known completely gone, she wasn't sure of anything anymore.

Then, there it was again—a quiet little knock, but definitely a knock. She suddenly found herself imagining that maybe it was Mr. Samuel Montford returning to take her out of this horrible place. Her heart began to beat faster. Perhaps he was so concerned for her welfare that he had found the courage to disobey her brother. He had already gone out of his way to furnish her cabin with finer things. Perhaps he knew how much distress she would feel upon waking up in this dark wilderness, and had now come back to rescue her and take her to safety.

Full of hope bred from desperation, she quickly unlatched the door and opened it. Her heart immediately sank in disappointment to see Jupiter standing there. She almost began to weep again.

Jupiter stood in perfect silence with his eyes on the ground, and waited nervously for her to speak.

Mary could see how awkward the situation was becoming so she swallowed her sorrow and said, "Good morning Jupiter. I assume you have come to prepare the fire?" Having servants around her at all times was something that she was accustomed to, and so she did not think twice about allowing Jupiter to enter the cabin. "Please come in," she said opening the door wider and stepping to one side.

Without a word, Jupiter went straight to the fireplace, crouched down and then began the task of building a fire. He was relieved that she did not seem upset or even mildly unnerved by his presence. Still, he decided that it would be best if he went about his tasks as quickly as possible, and spoke only when absolutely necessary.

Mary closed the door, and sat on a chair curiously watching the African as he worked. She remembered all of the strange things she had read about Africa in her books. Much of what she read seemed very unlikely. Although her protective upbringing had left her naïve in many ways, she was well aware that not all things printed in books were true.

But now, here she was in the presence of a real African. He could answer any questions she might have. Perhaps it was a good time to gather the wheat and burn the chaff on this matter. Mary looked at his broad back as he remained crouched at the fireplace. She decided that it was best just to ask him a question outright and said, "Jupiter, where in Africa were you born?"

Jupiter was hoping he could simply make the fire and go. The last thing he wanted was to talk with this woman, especially if she was going to ask foolish questions. Without turning his face from the fire that was now beginning to take hold of the kindling, he replied, "I was not born in Africa, My Lady." He hoped that this would put an end to her enquiries.

Mary was surprised by the deepness of his voice. She waited to see if he would say anything more, but he remained silent. Wanting to hear his voice again, she asked,

"Then were you born here, in America?"

"Yes, My Lady," he quickly said, as he added one more log to the now blazing fire. He then stood up, and turned towards Mary. Keeping his eyes averted, he said, "My Lady, I shall return with your breakfast shortly." Without another word, he walked over to the door and left.

Mary was disappointed that Jupiter would not be able to teach her about Africa. He also did not seem to like to talk at all, which was a change from her servants back in England. She wondered what his life as a slave must be like. Perhaps eventually, he would become more at ease and they could have a conversation. Mary dropped the bedcover from her shoulders and onto the bed. The fire had already begun to warm the cabin.

Happy to be outside in the open air, Jupiter sighed in relief. At least, she had not been frightened of him. That would have meant trouble, and could possibly have put his life in jeopardy. Actually, he had been quite surprised at how calm and relaxed she seemed around him.

As he walked toward the shack that housed both the kitchen and his bed, Jupiter wondered just how long he would be required to take care of this woman. Captain Springsteen told him nothing about when the job would end. Surely, they could not leave this young woman out here forever. Something would eventually have to change.

Jupiter entered the shack that was to be his temporary home. It consisted of one room with his trunk, a simple cot and washstand on one side. The kitchen area with a cooking stove was on the other. One of his responsibilities was to cook for the woman, and serve her meals.

As he began to prepare the breakfast, Jupiter worried about returning to the cabin. He did not want Mary to ask him any more questions. Speaking aloud to anyone had serious risks. It was true that he spoke with Captain Springsteen only when necessary. He definitely did not want to speak to this woman. All he wanted was to be able to go about his work in complete silence, and without any trouble.

Chapter 5

It had been almost three weeks since Mary arrived at the cabin. She accepted the fact that Jupiter did not want to answer any of her questions or to talk to her except when unavoidable, so for the most part she left him alone. The two had settled into a predictable and comfortable routine. The weather was rapidly getting warmer, and Mary no longer needed Jupiter to make a fire in the mornings or the evenings. The little contact she had with him was mainly when he was required to bring her food or fresh water.

The Duke had instructed that, as a part of her exile, Mary must do most of the necessary daily tasks including her own cleaning and laundry. He only ordered that all meals should be prepared for her, because he did not have confidence that she could properly cook and therefore feed herself. She was of no value to him if she were not to remain healthy and alive.

Compared to Mary's trip onboard the cargo ship, life in the wilderness did not seem too difficult for the first week. However, the repetitive daily chores and isolation started to weigh heavily on her. Increasingly, days seemed to drag on forever, and in the night it was not unusual for feelings of terrible loneliness to overwhelm her.

Adding to her misery was with intense worry she felt for her sister. Ann had always depended on Mary, who was like a mother to her. By nature, Ann was a timid girl and turned to her older sister whenever she was confused or frightened. How could she cope with being forced to marry William? How could she survive shackled every day to a man like him? Mary dreaded to think about it.

Jupiter was concerned about the woman's melancholy. He would often hear her weeping and praying inside the cabin when he passed by. Much to his relief, she never openly wept in front of him. He just hoped that her condition would not worsen. If it did then she would surely begin to take out her grief on him.

That particular morning, Mary finally had a reason to feel happy and hopeful. In just two days Mr. Montford would return, and she was eager to enjoy his company. The truth is that thoughts of the handsome Samuel Montford had kept her from falling into complete despair. Her daily dreams of walking and talking with this interesting gentleman helped her through the long and empty days. Mary was sure that Mr. Montford had found her intriguing, and when showing her the cabin he did happen to mention that he was widowed. In the past week, she increasingly found herself imagining all of the fascinating topics they could talk about when he returned, and was now anxious to finally have her fantasies realized.

Mary was tidying around the cabin, and thinking about all she could do to make the visit more pleasant. She opened the cupboard and took out one of her better dresses. All seven of the dresses that had been hastily packed in a trunk and sent with her were ill-suited to life in the wilderness, and some were already showing signs of wear. This one was still in almost perfect shape. It was a royal blue silk with white flower embroidery, and plenty of white-lace trim complimenting the sleeves and neckline. She looked at the lace on the arms and bodice of her gown. It had once been bright white, but now was dull grey. There were also ugly mud stains all around the hem. She began to panic. The anticipation of Mr. Montford's visit was the only thing that had kept her afloat over the past weeks, and it was important to her that she should look her best when he arrived.

Mary grabbed the dress in her arms and hurried outside to search for Jupiter. Perhaps he could help her. She spotted him near the barn chopping wood. As she quickly approached him, she noticed how finely dressed he looked even in the simple white shirt and breeches he was wearing. Jupiter must know what to do.

Mary abruptly stopped only an arms distance away. Jupiter looked at her and set down the axe. He could see that she was agitated, and he worried that the time had now come when he would have to pay the price for her grief.

"Jupiter, look at you!" she said in panic. At that moment, she almost lost control and wept out loud, but she knew it was important for her not to break down—not here and not now. Her eyes watered up, but no tears fell.

Jupiter was confused and began to wonder if living in the wilderness was perhaps too much of a strain on her. It was obvious that she was unaccustomed to hard living, and he had previously worried that she might lose her mind. The prospect being forced to care for a mad woman was frightening, and he would surely be blamed and punished for her derangement.

"Look at your shirt! It is so white!" she exclaimed, touching his sleeve for just a moment.

Jupiter wondered what she could be talking about. She was not making any sense, and now she had crossed an important boundary by touching his clothing.

Mary raised the dress she held in her arms and said, "In two days Mr. Montford will be returning, and the dress that I want to wear is in a terrible state. I realize that it is my responsibility to wash my own clothing, but I have done a horrible job of it. My dress, although I have washed it, does not look clean. Please Jupiter will you teach me how to get my clothes clean and bright like yours?"

Jupiter was very relieved that she had not lost her mind—at least she seemed to be making sense now. He thought for a moment about her request, and although he had been instructed not to do the washing for the woman, he had no orders that he could not teach her how to do washing. Certainly if doing this would make his life easier, it was best to just do it. "Yes My Lady," he simply answered.

Mary was so relieved to hear him agree to help her. This visit was the only thing that gave her any hope at all, and it was very important that she look her best. She wanted more than anything to make a good impression on Samuel Montford. "Oh thank you Jupiter!" she exclaimed.

Jupiter felt uncomfortable by her expression of gratitude. She should not be thanking him for anything at any time. If she continued to do this, it could cause a great deal of trouble for him.

That day, Jupiter taught Mary the tricks to washing clothing and removing stains. She was amazed at just how complicated such a seemingly simple task could be. After they had finished cleaning the blue dress and hanging it to dry, Jupiter also helped her with some of her other laundry.

As they worked together, Mary thought that she would try to find out more about Samuel Montford by asking questions of Jupiter. She was disappointed when he either could not or would not provide her with sufficient answers. After a few of attempts to find out more about the man, she finally gave up and accepted that she would have to learn about Mr. Montford from the man himself.

For Jupiter, Mary's questions made it clear that she had a romantic interest in Montford. This was very good news for him. If Montford would want to marry the woman, then she would certainly no longer be required to live in this cabin, and he would no longer be required to serve her. The sooner that happened, the sooner he could return to his ordinary life with Springsteen.

Thinking it was in his best interest to help Mary make a good impression on Montford, Jupiter offered to prepare some sweet cakes for the visit. He also silently planned how he would set out the table in the grassy shade of two mature trees that grew not far from the cabin. Surely such a setting could only help to hasten a marriage proposal.

That evening, when Jupiter came to the cabin and placed Mary's supper on the table in front of her, she smiled at him and said, "Thank you for your kindness today Jupiter. You have helped me to avoid a terrible embarrassment."

This was yet another expression of open gratitude, and it made Jupiter very nervous. "My Lady, I am a slave. You do not thank a slave," he said, while looking at the floor.

"I thank anyone who is willing to help me and show me mercy, and that would include slaves," said Mary defiantly.

Jupiter did not say a word, but bowed and went out the door. As he walked in the cool night air, he hoped that she would have the sense not thank him in front of Montford. Such a thing would only mean trouble for him.

Chapter 6

The day that Mr. Montford was to arrive, Mary woke early in anticipation. The sun was rising and the light was coming through the thin curtains on the window. She wrapped herself in the blanket and went out on the porch to call Jupiter, who she knew would be in the barn doing his morning chores.

"Jupiter!" she called. She saw him stick his head out of the barn. "Could you please make a fire this morning, and bring me lots of water. I need your assistance to prepare a bath."

Jupiter did not question her request to make a bath. This had not been mentioned as one of his duties of care, but today he was feeling even more hopeful that Montford might marry her, and was willing to do anything that could help this happen quickly.

Mary sat silently at the table eating her breakfast and reading her Bible, while Jupiter made preparations for her bath. He dragged an old copper bathtub from outside and placed it in the middle of the room while the water heated over the fire. After the bath was prepared, he did not say a word, but simply walked out the door closing it behind him.

At first, Mary was not sure if Jupiter was finished as he said nothing when he left. She looked out the window and saw him returning to his shack. She then quickly undressed and slipped into the warm water. The small, cramped bathtub could not compare to the long marble bath she had enjoyed in

England, but at that moment it seemed like the greatest luxury on earth.

She would have stayed in the water all morning if she was not quickly driven out by its cooling temperature. After drying off, she threw her shift over her naked body, and looked at her clothing that she had previously laid out on the bed. Thanks to Jupiter's help, the stains on her dress were gone and the lace was once again a bright white. She then stared at the stays that lay beside the gown. Since her journey on the ship, she had abandoned the stays as they were impossible to fasten properly without help.

Mary hesitated to call for Jupiter, but he really was her only option. And with Mr. Montford arriving today, she was determined to look her best.

Before he left Captain Springsteen had tactfully explained that Jupiter was not the sort of man that women needed to be worried about, and as she had known many such men in the courts of England, she did not have difficulty understanding what he meant by this. Mary went to the door of the cabin and called for Jupiter.

When Jupiter arrived, she explained to him, as best she could, how she needed his assistance. Jupiter was trained as a gentleman's servant and was accustomed to private and personal servitude, but to assist a woman was different. First of all, he knew nothing about stays and was nervous about what it could entail. If it was a choice, he would have refused her request and walked away. However, he could not risk upsetting her especially with Montford arriving today. He consoled himself by remembering that by helping her with this garment it may speed up a marriage proposal from Mr. Montford.

Jupiter was waiting on the porch when she came out in only her shift and holding the stays loosely around her middle. She turned with her back to him and grabbed hold of the porch post with one of her arms. "Now Jupiter, just pull the laces very tight and then tie them so that they will not come loose," she said matter of fact.

43

Jupiter was confused and uncomfortable with her instructions. He pulled the laces although not with much force as he was afraid of hurting her.

"Just a wee bit tighter," she instructed.

Against his better judgment, Jupiter pulled them tighter. Mary winced slightly and for a moment he feared that he was in terrible trouble. But instead of being angry, as he expected, she happily said, "Perfect, now please tie the laces tightly so they will not come loose." Jupiter did as she asked.

Mary then turned and ran her hands down her secured front. "Thank you Sir," she cheerfully chirped, and then went into the cabin and closed the door.

Jupiter stepped down from the porch and walked towards his shed. He hoped again that she would not thank him or call him 'sir' in front of Mr. Montford. Thinking of the stays, he simply shook his head in bewilderment. "So that is why most white women are so angry and mean," he said to himself.

Mary sat at the table under the shade of the large trees, and waited anxiously for Mr. Montford's arrival. She was pleasantly surprised when Jupiter had asked her if he should set up the table and chairs outside. This was something she had not thought about doing, and now was so pleased that they would be having tea in the open air. It would be much more pleasant than in the darkness of the little cabin, and she had to confess to herself, much more romantic.

She brought the Bible outside with her so that she would have something to do while waiting. It was also true that she had thought about how her reading the Bible in such a lovely setting would make a pleasant sight for Mr. Montford when he rode up. It was very important that she make the best impression possible as their time together was so limited.

Mary placed the book in front of her and opened it to a random page,

Come, my beloved, let us go forth into the field; let us lodge in the villages. Let us get up early to the vineyards; let us see if the vine flourish, whether the tender grape appear, and the pomegranates bud forth: there will I give thee my loves.

She was amazed that of all the pages she could have turned to, it was this one. Could God being trying to tell her that Mr. Samuel Montford was to be her chosen bridegroom? Could it be that the Hand of God had brought her here to the wilderness, just for that reason? She looked up from her book and saw Jupiter going from the barn to the shack carrying a bowl of eggs. He was fully dressed with a coat, waistcoat and hat. Mary was very pleased to see that he was putting in an extra effort for Mr. Montford's visit. She wanted everything to be perfect.

When Mr. Montford finally did arrive, it was not as Mary had hoped. She had imagined him finding her looking picture perfect while sitting at the table, and reading under the shade of the trees. But waiting for him for so long made her nervous, and she found herself needing to use the outhouse. This is where she was when she heard the wagon finally roll in. As she hurried out from behind the cabin, she saw that the horse reigns had been tied to the tree, and Jupiter was already unloading the supplies. Also, much to her disappointment, Mr. Pierce had come along. She had been hoping to have the company of Mr. Montford alone.

Still, she tried to hide both her embarrassment and disappointment, and with brave cheer approached her guests. "Mr. Montford and Mr. Pierce, how lovely to see you again," she said smiling warmly.

The men looked very pleased to see her. They both removed their hats and bowed in greeting.

"Lady Mary," said Montford, wanting to edge Pierce out as much as he could, "what a pleasure to finally be able to see you again. I notice that you have set out a wonderful place in the shade for us to enjoy this fine afternoon."

Without another word, Montford offered Mary his arm which she gladly took. They then walked toward the table and chairs with Pierce unhappily following behind.

"And Captain Springsteen? Is he not joining us today?" Mary asked.

"No My Lady," interjected Pierce, before Montford could answer. "Captain Springsteen has gone to the secure some minor problems with the enemy in the north, and we do not know when he will be back."

Jupiter, who was bringing a third chair to the table, overheard the conversation about his master. He knew that Springsteen was often sent into dangerous situations, and sometimes worried about him being killed. If Springsteen were to die, where would that leave him? Although familiar with most of the Captain's business, he had never seen his master's will. This caused him concern.

Montford took the chair from Jupiter and offered it to Mary. Pierce was feeling frustrated, but tried not to show it. He resented the fact that he was not single and in a position to openly court the woman. It had become clear to him that Montford was beginning to entertain the possibility that he could marry into The Vine. Pierce balked at this idea as he considered Montford too weak and soft to father worthy children. He, on the other hand, would make a far more suitable candidate. If only she would send a signal of love his way, he would quickly ensure his widowhood to take his rightful place within The Holy Family.

After Mary was seated, the two men sat down on the chairs that were facing opposite each other. Mary politely smiled at one man and then the other. She clasped her hands on the table in front of her and said, "I certainly hope that all goes well with Captain Springsteen, and that he returns soon."

"How much do you know about the war, My Lady?" asked Montford, wondering if she had any knowledge that he could use to his advantage.

Mary knew that this was a delicate subject, and immediately thought it best to keep what she did know to herself. "I know very little," she said. "But it is mostly finished, from what I have heard, and is really a concern of men. I prefer to talk of the kinds of things that make women happy." She then noticed how Samuel Montford's blue waist coat matched his eyes, making them all the more striking.

Although her response was not what Montford had hoped for, he found that he was not very bothered by it. He was far too busy enjoying the way in which she looked at him. Since women were meant to be a distraction from the everyday burdens of men anyway, it was, in fact, better that she had nothing to say on the matter. This woman was definitely a charming distraction. He leaned in towards Mary and responded by asking playfully, "And My Lady, what is it that makes women happy?"

Mary felt a warmth flow throughout her body and thought that she could not have been happier than at that moment. Finally, here was someone she could converse with openly and honestly. Merciful God had not abandoned her, but instead had brought her a handsome and charming gentleman. This day was going to be better than she ever imagined it would be.

Determined to create a lasting connection with Mr. Montford, Mary decided that this was a good time to begin to share the more personal philosophical thoughts she had been having in the last few weeks. Within her daily battle with despair, she had been thinking a great deal about the idea of happiness. She had also spent much time searching the only book at her disposable for anything that could help clarify the meaning of the word. Perhaps it was best to begin any discussion on the subject with a quotation. Eager to share her ideas and open the way for a stimulating conversation, she picked up the Bible that was still on the table, opened it to a marked page and replied, "I have searched for an understanding of happiness and have found these words,

Pride goeth before destruction, and a haughty spirit before a fall. Better it is to be of a humble spirit with the lowly, than to divide the spoil with the proud. He that handleth a matter wisely shall find good: and whoso trusteth in the LORD, happy is he.

So I assume that within this message is perhaps an important part to finding happiness for both sexes."

Immediately after she spoke, Mary saw that Montford and Pierce were visibly uncomfortable. This was not the reaction she was expecting. She had been hopeful that her words would open an interesting and enlightening dialogue—at least with Mr. Montford. Instead, both of the men looked at her with that mild blend of fear and hostility that she knew all too well. It was suddenly painfully clear that she had been naïve and foolish to think that she could be open and honest with either of these men. Her position in exile was even far more vulnerable than that in England, and she must do nothing to antagonize those who held power. She was sadly awakened to the realization that, to ensure her best chances of survival, she would have to protect her real self and play the role that these men expected.

Thinking fast she added, "But I suppose that mainly women do find happiness in all of the finer things such as beautiful clothes, good food, and charming company." Mary watched her strategy work as the men's faces began to relax again into confident smiles.

"And certainly one of the things that makes a man happy is the company of a beautiful woman, Lady Mary," said Montford, trying to seize the opportunity to charm her again. He was certain that it was working.

Pierce wished that he could be as openly flirtatious, but held back fearing that it would be considered inappropriate and would only result in making him look bad. He felt increasingly frustrated that Montford seemed to have his sights set on courting the woman, and that his own marriage prevented him from competing on an equal footing.

"And how is Jupiter behaving? Do you require him to be disciplined while we are here?" asked Pierce, hoping at a chance to use the whip he had brought along with him.

Mary smiled, "Gentlemen, you should be commended for finding such an excellent servant. My brother had given you a difficult task, but you have met the challenge, proving your worthiness," she said, being careful to give the praise to these men and not to Jupiter. She realized that his position was even more vulnerable than her own, and did not want to say anything that could accidentally encourage Pierce's apparent thirst for brutality.

Jupiter approached the table with the tea tray, and for a moment all eyes were on him. As he served the tea and sweets, he was relieved that Mary only spoke to him to convey an order. She never added 'please' or 'thank you' at the end of any requests. This had been a real worry for Jupiter. He knew that Pierce had a serious reputation for the harsh discipline of slaves, and would be looking for any reason to flog him. On top of that, Jupiter could see that Pierce, like Montford, wanted this woman. This made him even more dangerous.

The visit continued to go smoothly enough, and Mary kept her deep disappointment hidden. She had spent the past weeks imagining a different Mr. Montford. The real one was not highly intelligent, witty or interesting like the one she had dreamed up in her mind. With all the hardship and isolation that she had endured, she had created a fantasy that provided her with hope and kept despair temporarily at bay. Now her life sustaining fantasy had been dashed to pieces by the real Samuel Montford.

Still, she kept smiling throughout the visit. She must seem happy and pleased with the company as there was no other choice. All afternoon she chattered on about subjects of no interest to her. From the outside, she made it look as if it was a pleasure instead of the horrible chore it was proving to be. However, this was nothing entirely new to her as she had often been required to provide similar acts back in England.

The long afternoon hours dragged on in trivial conversation. Both men tried as best they could to impress Mary. Montford practiced his flirtatious charm, and used everything he had learned from his British education. Pierce, on the other hand, talked endlessly of his land and business to the point where even he began to wonder if he were being a little boorish.

At last Mary had taken all she could of the tedium, and decided that it was a suitable time to put an end to it the way she usually put an end to many a dull conversation. Raising her fingers gracefully to her mouth, she yawned.

"Please excuse me gentlemen," she smiled apologetically. "I am afraid that the burden and strain of my exile has left me weakened. I now seem to require far more rest than I have ever needed before."

Montford could see that Mary was tired, although he didn't guess that it was from boredom. Keeping to his gallant image, he responded, "Of course My Lady, I assume none of this has been easy for you. We can certainly understand how you would be so fatigued."

Pierce knew that he could never match Montford's charm or good looks, but was feeling confident that he had greatly impressed Mary with all that he had to offer. Self-assured that she would be anticipating his return, he said, "Lady Mary, Mr. Montford and I should go now so that you may get your rest. I wish we could return sooner than three weeks, but unfortunately our hands are tied."

Montford was not happy that Pierce was including himself in the next visit. He had tried to keep him from coming along this time, but Pierce was absolutely persistent. In the beginning, he thought that Pierce's marriage would surely keep him from entertaining ambitions about The Vine, but now he could see that he was wrong. Montford knew that next time he must not fail in keeping him from tagging along.

Happy that they would finally leave her in peace, Mary smiled at the men and said, "This has been a wonderful afternoon, gentlemen, and I do thank you for staying and keeping me company for such a long time. It is a terrible thing for a woman to be alone."

She then made a move as if to rise from her chair, and Montford leapt to his feet to assist her. Pierce did not like that Montford responded to her gesture before he had a chance. It left him with nothing else to do other than respectfully stand. As Mary rose from her chair, she saw Pierce's eyes drag down the front of her bodice. His look left her feeling sickened, and she had to quickly turn away to hide her reaction.

Jupiter was already hitching up the horses to the wagon. From what he could see and hear, the meeting had gone very well. It was difficult to tell how long it might be before the woman married Mr. Montford. For now with Captain Springsteen away, it wasn't so urgent, but he still wished it could move quickly. Certainly, if Mr. Pierce kept insisting on joining them, it could take much longer.

As they were preparing to leave, Montford took Mary's hand and gently kissed it. He looked as warmly and sincerely into her eyes as he could and said, "Lady Mary, it has been my greatest honour to have spent the afternoon with such a noble and gracious lady."

Mary looked at his handsome genteel face, and for a brief moment the old hope flickered—just for a moment, she felt like maybe she was wrong. Maybe he was something more like the man that she had imagined him to be. But then, she thought about the afternoon and the things that he had said. It was clear that fearful desperation was once again creating illusions, and she had to face reality. This Mr. Montford was not, nor would he ever be the one she had dreamed of.

Pierce also took the liberty of kissing her hand when he said farewell. She felt that his lips lingered there just a little too long, and his grin when he looked up at her, made her very uncomfortable.

The two men climbed up into the wagon, and Jupiter handed Mr. Montford the reigns. Montford stared at Jupiter for a moment, and then said to Mary, "My Lady, if you are in dire need of entertainment then have Jupiter sing for you. He is one of the finest singers you will ever hear."

Mary looked at Jupiter, whose eyes never left the ground as if he had not heard his name at all. "Thank you Mr. Montford. I shall remember that." Mary smiled and waved as the men drove off. She sighed in relief after their wagon turned the bend. Having waited so impatiently for the arrival of her company, she was now savoring the freedom she felt at their departure.

When she turned around to look for Jupiter, he had disappeared. She quietly went into the cabin, and removed her dress. She then reached behind to the laces of the stays. Feeling increasingly frustrated and angry at how long it was taking to pull them loose, she began to cry and tear at them frantically. Finally after a great deal of work, she was able to rip them completely from her body and in that single action tossed them across the room. They landed in the fireplace raising a small cloud of dusty ash. Taking in a long deep breath, she ran her hands down her tired sore rib cage. At that point, she realized how completely exhausted she really was. Mary then curled up on her bed, and fell into a deep sleep.

She was sitting in the family pew in Westminster Abbey. It was very dim and dark, and everything was silent. Mary knew that she was there to see a wedding, although the church seemed empty of people. She looked to her left, and saw Ann sitting beside her. A least she thought it was Ann, but could not tell for certain because there was a thick black veil hiding the girl's face. Mary felt afraid, but was unsure why.

Then suddenly, she found herself walking down the church aisle and became aware that it was her own wedding that was happening. The organ grinded out a sad horrible tune, and somewhere a woman was wailing. The pews were filled to capacity, but she recognized no one. As she walked down the aisle, she was horrified to realize that she had forgotten to put on her bridal gown, and was entirely naked. Mary wanted to run out of the church, but the Archbishop of Canterbury was at the alter calling to her to hurry, and she could not find the courage to defy him.

As the guests in the pews stared at her, she tried to hide her nakedness with the large bouquet of white roses that she carried, but the petals of the flowers kept falling away. She approached the altar, and saw Samuel Montford there waiting for her. Immediately, she knew that it was he who had arranged for this marriage. She tried to tell him that she must go back for her dress, but he insisted that if they pretended she was wearing one, no one would notice. She knew he was wrong, but could do nothing more about it.

Mary saw that the Archbishop was ready to perform the ceremony. She looked again at her groom, and was horrified to see James Pierce now standing beside her. He stared at her with his usual sickly grin. She was terrified and ready to run, but just then, the Archbishop announced that the doors had been locked and no one could leave. Filled with overwhelming anxiety and fear, Mary suddenly awoke in a cold sweat, her heart fluttering like a wounded bird.

At first, she did not know where she was, but then she looked around the room and sadly recognized her log prison. The sun was beginning to set, which made the dull grey walls of the cabin seem that much greyer. She noticed the table and three of the chairs were missing. It was then that she recalled the miserable and disappointing afternoon she had endured.

Why could Mr. Montford not have been different? It would have been so wonderful had he been the man she had imagined. Why did it seem as if not only her brother, but God too punished her? She stared into the darkness of the ceiling above her and prayed:

O God, you are my God, earnestly I seek you; my soul thirsts for you, my body longs for you, in a dry and weary land where there is no water.

Sitting up on her bed, Mary was suddenly struck by a feeling of hunger. It was well past the time she usually had her supper. Quickly getting dressed, she hurried out to find Jupiter. As she approached the shack, she could see him stirring something in a pot that hung over an open fire. The closer she got, the more she could smell the delicious aroma of the stew. It warmed her hungry body, and seemed to restore her spirit a little.

There was an old stump not far from the fire where Mary sat down. For a while, she said nothing and simply enjoyed the warmth and the silence. Finally, her hunger got the best of her and she asked, "Will it be ready soon?"

"Yes My Lady, it is ready now," Jupiter answered, keeping his eyes only on the cooking pot.

Mary looked at the distant pine trees. The strange light of the setting sun bathed them in an unusual green glow. "That is wonderful news," she said. "I believe that sleep has left me completely famished."

She watched as Jupiter began to slice bread on an old rustic table that was sitting beside the fire. Mary suddenly wondered what it must be like for him having to live here. Like her, he was completely alone with no one to talk to. What does he worry and dream about? How much does he resent having to serve her every day? Although he never said or did anything to outwardly indicate this resentment, Mary knew that this must be the way he felt. What else could he feel as a slave? Anyone in that same position would have to feel that way. Yet despite what he must feel, he always took good care of her. Mary felt grateful for that. As she contemplated their strange relationship, she began to think that, as he took on the duty of caring for her, perhaps then the Laws of God demanded that it was her duty to take care of him. She smiled and said, "Please let me know if there is anything you require that I may pass on the request to Mr. Montford the next time he returns."

Knowing that it was certainly not his place to ever request anything, Jupiter simply tried to put the issue to rest by replying, "Yes My Lady."

Mary confused him again when she said, "Do not worry at the moment about returning the table and chairs to the cabin. I wish to eat here."

Jupiter did not say a word, but instead picked up the rose covered china bowl that was nearby and ladled the stew into it. He placed the bowl on a supper plate with a slice of bread and a silver spoon. With his eyes looking only at the plate in his hand, he held it out to her. When she took the bowl in her hands, she looked directly at his face, but he never returned the gaze.

"Thank you, Jupiter," she said, tasting a small amount of the hot stew. "Please, would you pour yourself a bowl and eat with me. I would rather not eat alone tonight."

Jupiter did not want to eat with this woman, but he had no choice. Disobeying her could mean punishment, and without Springsteen around, any punishment would likely be done by Pierce. He ladled some stew into his own wooden bowl, picked up his wooden spoon, and sat down on a log about three yards away. He did not look anywhere except at the stew, and slowly began to eat.

Mary looked at him and smiled, "Jupiter, I realize that you are uncomfortable eating with me, so thank you for staying. It is just that I cannot be alone at this time."

Jupiter was surprised that the woman seemed so unhappy. He knew that she had been looking forward to Montford's visit and believed that, other than the problem of Pierce showing up, the visit seemed to go very well. Mr. Montford was obviously extremely fond of her, so why was she like this? Perhaps, it was just that she was missing him now that he was gone. Jupiter still held out hope that the woman would marry soon, and he would be returned to his regular life.

The evening was warm and the setting sun continued to bring the colors of the world into vivid focus. Other than the sounds of birds calling for each other, everything was calm and still. Mary was thankful for the small mercy of Jupiter's silent company. She took a mouthful of bread and thought to herself, *a time to keep silent, and a time to speak.*

Chapter 7

The following morning Jupiter prepared Mary's breakfast as usual, and carried it to the cabin. He knocked on the door, but there was no response. He knocked a little louder, and a muffled voice from inside said something that was unclear. Jupiter was confused, and paused for a moment. When he heard no further sound, he slowly opened the door and peered in. Mary was not sitting at the table in wait for her breakfast as she usually was. Instead, she remained in her bed with the covers pulled completely over her head.

He walked in and set the tray down. Expecting that she would soon roll out of bed and come to the table, he then pulled out her chair and waited. Still, she did not move. Jupiter began to wonder if she was well. He thought about saying something, but what could he say? It was not his place to say anything. He glanced at the bed, and did see her move a little under the white cover. Finally, he realized that there was no point in waiting there any longer. If she was going to ignore him like this, it surely meant that she just wanted him to leave. He left the chair where it was, and turned to go do other chores.

In about two hours' time, he returned as usual to collect the dishes. He knocked, but this time she did not respond at all. Again, he slowly opened the door. The breakfast was still sitting on the table, just as he had left it. He looked at the bed, and could see that Mary remained completely buried under the covers. Jupiter was suddenly struck with the fear that she really could have taken ill or even worse. Hesitating to break the silence in the room, but knowing he must say something, Jupiter asked, "My Lady is there a problem with your breakfast?"

Mary pulled the blankets from her head. Her hair was disheveled and her eyes were red. She certainly looked like she was ill. "I have no appetite today," she said curtly, and then turned towards the wall.

Jupiter was beginning to get very worried. If she was seriously ill, what should he do about it? What if she died? He would surely be blamed and most likely accused of murder. Fearing for his own future, he asked, "Are you ill, My Lady?"

"I do not believe so Jupiter. I am just very sad," she said, with her back still to him.

"Can I bring you something, My Lady," he said, hoping that he could find an easy solution to this problem. He glanced at the fireplace, and noticed the stays lying in the ashes. This was not a good sign.

For Mary, the darkness seemed to be pouring in all around her. Yesterday morning she had happily awakened with so much hope, but yesterday was gone forever. Today the world was nothing but a bleak and horrible place. Could there be anything at all worth living for? If there was, she could not see it. What reason was there to be continually struggling through the dirty mire of existence, when there was no relief in sight? It was a wicked world full of wicked people—it was *a land as dark as darkness itself.*

Feeling like she just needed to hang on to anything to keep herself from being swallowed by the threatening pit, Mary hugged the blankets tightly. She closed her eyes, and said a silent prayer, *Oh God, save me from the lion's mouth: for thou hast heard me from the horns of the unicorns.*

Suddenly, like a tiny flicking light she remembered what Montford had told her about Jupiter's singing. At home, music had often been the one thing that could make her feel whole again whenever life seemed hopelessly empty—and never before had she faced such hopeless emptiness as at this very moment.

She turned back to face Jupiter, and propped herself up on one elbow. "Mr. Montford said that you are a very good singer. Could you please sing a song for me Jupiter?" she pleaded. "It has been months since I have heard any music at all, and it may be the only medicine that can save me."

Jupiter did not want to sing in front of this woman. He did not like to sing in front of anyone at all. Singing was private for him. It was one of the only things that belonged exclusively to him and when he was forced to share it, it made him feel like something precious was being stolen. Still, this woman was so sad that she could not even eat. He knew that he would have to try something to keep the situation from getting worse. Jupiter looked at the grey ashes in the fireplace and began to sing.

Oh Lord, in the morning hear me cry
Oh Lord in the morning hear me cry
Oh Lord in the morning hear me cry
What is hidden from sight,
 Bring into the light.

Oh Lord in the evening hear me cry
Oh Lord in the evening hear me cry
Oh Lord in the evening hear me cry
What is hidden from sight,
 Bring into the light.

Mary could not believe how beautiful Jupiter sang. She had heard many renowned singers in England, but none could compare to him. As he sung the verses over again, she watched his face transform from the stolid mask he usually wore, to a man filled with such a degree of life that it left her in awe. Could the face of Moses have shone any brighter when his veil was lifted?

The oppressive darkness that had been crushing her slowly began to lift from her spirit. Then suddenly without warning, she felt herself overcome by a myriad of strange and powerful emotions! A force she had never felt before swept down upon her like a million demon-angels! She was knocked back onto the bed, and rendered completely helpless! She began to tremble, and primal weeping sounds were flying from her lips! Without any hesitation, Mary completely surrendered to the power that now possessed her. Although a terrible fury seemed to have taken over her body, her mind and soul rested in a calm and loving peacefulness beyond anything she had ever imagined possible.

When Jupiter saw Mary fall back on the bed, and heard her begin to sob hysterically, he fell silent. He was terrified! What had happened? What had he done? Had his singing made everything worse? What would he do if she descended into complete madness? Without a word, he ran out the door, and into his shack. There, he sat nervously upon his cot and worried about what he should do next. This was not good at all. The woman was going completely mad and he didn't know how to stop it.

Shortly after Jupiter left, the intense vision of peace that encompassed her slowly subsided and then vanished. Mary just lay on her bed, not wanting to move. She wanted only to remember that place of love she had entered. A smile came across her face, as she realized that she had been shown something special. Something that, although now gone, had not left her completely. A piece of it had lodged in her heart, and she knew that it could never be removed. She took in a deep breath, and sat up.

Mary then thought about Jupiter, and worried about how she must have frightened him. He had been so kind to sing for her when she asked. What must he now be thinking? She knew that she must try and explain things, which would not be easy considering that she did not quite understand it herself.

Mary got out of her bed, and ate what part of her breakfast was still fresh enough to eat. She then washed and dressed before going outside to look for Jupiter. As soon as she went around the cabin, she could see him diligently piling freshly cut wood near the barn. Mary walked quickly towards him.

Jupiter heard her approaching from behind, but kept working. He did not turn around because he was afraid of what he might see.

"Jupiter," she softly called.

Reluctantly, Jupiter turned and looked briefly at her. He was very relieved to see that she was properly dressed, and her hair had been tucked neatly under a bonnet. Perhaps, she would not go mad after all.

"Jupiter, I am so very sorry for my outburst," she said sincerely. "You must know that you did nothing wrong. Some things are just God's Will, and we have no control. I too was surprised by what happened. Please know, however, that your song did restore me, and I deeply thank you for that. Truly, dear Jupiter, it saved me. I have never heard such beautiful music before. It was as if it came straight from Heaven." Mary paused for a moment as she remembered the song. "I just needed to let you know that I am sorry if I frightened you," she said, hoping that Jupiter would understand. "And also to assure you that I am not succumbing to insanity which is what you must be thinking."

Jupiter was surprised by how calm and sane she sounded after what he had just seen. He was definitely feeling less fearful that she would break down completely. However, the way she was talking to him now made him more fearful about other things. This was not the type of exchange he should be having with her. There were boundaries to be maintained, and his survival had always depended upon keeping those boundaries well in place.

"My Lady, you do not apologize to a slave," he said, looking at the ground and hoping the matter would end there.

After everything that had happened, these words cut straight into Mary's heart. The previous day she had suffered an entire afternoon playing a foolish masquerade with the men who claimed they were her friends, but in reality were her jail guards.

She could no longer stomach any more deceitful games. Why should she not just be upfront and honest with Jupiter? What consequences could come of speaking the truth out here in the wilderness? After all, were they both not prisoners together?

Mary took a deep breath, and then began to release everything that was on her mind. "First Sir, I will say that you are not my slave, and in the Eyes of God you are no one's slave. The truth is that I abhor slavery, and consider it an abomination in the Sight of God. I do not say so in front of Mr. Montford or Mr. Pierce because I know it would do no good, and only make my situation as well as yours much more difficult. Like you, I must watch what I say, and give people what they want to believe. Not to do so is precisely why I am here now—banished to the wilderness."

Mary could see the look of fear on Jupiter's face, and realized just how much he did not trust her. Determined to try to make him see her, she looked him straight in the eye in a way that forced him to look at her. "Please know," she said, "that as I did yesterday, I will continue to never reveal my true feelings about slavery, nor betray you by treating you with human decency in the presence of Mr. Montford, or Mr. Pierce, or anyone else who has power over you. You need not worry about that. But in their absence, I will certainly treat you in a way that God intended you to be treated. That is my duty to God, to myself, and to you who, the same as I, was created in the Image of God. Therefore, when the situation calls for it, I will say 'sorry' or 'thank you' or 'please' and you had simply better get used to it."

Jupiter listened in bewilderment. He could not believe that this woman was speaking to him like this. A moment ago, he was almost certain that she had regained her sanity. Now, he was having doubts again.

For Mary, the words she had held in for so long just continued to flow out of her mouth, and she was enjoying the feeling of relief as she surrendered to them. "Also," she added, "whether or not either one of us like this situation that we are in, we are stuck with it. For the most part, we have gotten along very well, but most women have a need to speak and speak often. Although some men find this less than desirable, it is an important part of our womanhood, and when we must live in silence for too long, it is a heavy burden to carry. So I will not insist that you respond in kind or that, as a man, you completely understand, but I would ask that you at least allow me to talk to you as I would to anyone. And even if you do not listen fully to all I have to say, at least have the courtesy to answer honestly any question I may ask of you."

Jupiter was at a loss what to think. For years, he had managed to keep a safe distance from other people, and had certainly mastered his role when it came to white people. Now, this strange woman was trying to change the rules. He did not want the uncertainty that would come with this new arrangement, but what choice did he have? Confused about what else to say or do, he simply replied, "Yes, My Lady."

"Wonderful!" responded Mary, bringing her hands together as if in prayer. "Today, we begin anew! From this point onward, when you bring me my meals, you shall also bring one for yourself, and then we shall dine together. What a blessing it will be, not to have to eat in lonely silence again."

Jupiter did not reply. He did not know what to say or do. He couldn't just defy her, but to follow along with her request was to jeopardize everything. It would be wrong, and very uncomfortable for him to sit down with this woman at her table. What good could possibly come of this? With no conceivable way out of the situation, Jupiter just stood still and continued to say nothing.

Filled with her new faith, Mary simply accepted the silence to mean that he was willing to try this new arrangement. "I shall look forward to seeing you again at supper, and please ensure that you bring with you two china plates and the appropriate silverware. No one eats from a wooden bowl at my table," she said, then turned and headed back to the cabin.

With each step Mary took, she thought of her brother Charles, and how he had sent her here to crush her spirit once and for all. For a short time, the victory was almost his, but she was determined not to let that happen again. Mary was realizing that, if she desired it, the power was in her own hands. If she could fully embrace God's Truth, and search for what she needed to strengthen her own heart, she would win this war, and her brother would be defeated.

When she stepped into the cabin, she looked at the fireplace and her stays that lay like a decomposing carcass in the ashes. Her ribs were still sore from wearing them. Taking the poker that leaned against the stones, she at first just prodded the stays, making little dust clouds. Then she quickly slipped the poker underneath, and lifted them from the fireplace. Walking out the door, she carried them to the back of the cabin and swinging the poker forward, she tossed the stays as far as she could into some dense bush.

She looked at where she had thrown them, and could see only a bit of grey ash on some leaves. *"To loose the bands of wickedness, to undo the heavy burdens, to let the oppressed go free, and to break every yoke,"* she said aloud, and then turned and went back into the cabin.

Chapter 8

Mary sat at the table and waited anxiously for Jupiter to arrive. She was a little worried that he may have had second thoughts about dining with her. She was also extremely hungry. When she saw Jupiter at the open door with the tray in hand, she immediately said, "I am so glad that you are here. Please come in Jupiter."

Without a word, Jupiter walked in and placed the tray of food on the table. Mary was relieved to see that he had brought with him two dinner plates. Without thinking, she hungrily grabbed one of the plates, and placed it in front of her. She then looked up at Jupiter, who stood silently waiting.

"Oh Jupiter, you promised you would dine with me, so please sit down. You do not have to ever wait for me to ask you," said Mary smiling. She happily picked up her fork and began to eat a little too quickly.

Jupiter slowly sat down across from her. This new arrangement made things very uncomfortable for him. Carefully, he took the second plate of food from the tray. He then picked up a fork and moved around some of the potatoes. At this point, he could not bring himself to put anything to his mouth.

Mary felt like she was filled with a new kind of energy. She continued to throw decorum to the wind and eat with vigor. "I apologize, Jupiter, for being so rude, but I cannot tell you how desperate I become when I get this hungry. And you, Sir, are an excellent chef," she said between bites.

Jupiter did not respond, but instead began to eat slowly. He was still having a difficult time finding his appetite.

Mary looked up from her almost empty plate and noticed how Jupiter had barely touched his food. It was not going to be a simple matter to make him feel comfortable around her, but she was not going to give up easily. "So Sir, you say that you were born in America?" she asked, hoping to persuade him to talk.

"Yes," replied Jupiter, who kept his eyes on his plate.

She was disappointed by his abrupt answer, but was determined to press on. "And where exactly in America were you born?"

"North Carolina," he replied, still keeping his eyes averted.

"Well, I have studied maps of America so I do know where North Carolina is. I am still not exactly sure where I am, but I suspect North Carolina is close. Is it close Jupiter?" asked Mary, hoping that he would soon become more talkative.

"It is due south of here," replied Jupiter.

Mary was determined more than ever that the conversation would continue. "And were your parents born in North Carolina as well, and are they still there?"

Jupiter had stopped eating, and was now just dragging his fork around the food again. "I do not have a mother or a father."

Mary looked at him curiously. "But everyone has a mother and a father. You could not have just dropped from the sky," she said.

"What I mean is that I never knew my mother or my father," replied Jupiter, a little annoyed that maybe she was thinking he was simple.

"Well then, who raised you?" asked Mary. She was pleased that now he was giving more than one word answers, but knew that he would still not volunteer much information without encouragement.

"There was a woman named Martha who took care of me when I was very young. She worked in the kitchen." He looked up at Mary for just a moment, and then quickly back down at his food. He could not remember the last time he had spoken Martha's name out loud. It sounded strange to say it again.

Mary was beginning to suspect that asking Jupiter too many questions at once could drive him away. She decided it was best if she changed the subject to herself and her own life. "I do know who my parents were, although they are both now dead," she said. "I have very little memory of my father as he was rarely at home. I know that he was tall, or at least he seemed that way. I suppose that I was very short at the time, so perhaps he was not that tall." Mary laughed a little, but Jupiter remained stoically staring at his food. "I cannot remember him ever speaking directly to me. In some ways, he was just like a ghost I would sometimes see at mealtimes or in the hallway. He died when I was eight years old. There were whispers about the circumstances of his death, and as a child I overheard things that made me believe it may have been murder."

Jupiter looked briefly at Mary, who appeared deep in the past as she stared down at the table. He never really thought much about this woman or what her life was like before coming here. He purposely tried not to think too much about anyone at all if it did not directly concern him. It was better that way. Staying focused only on the task at hand had always been essential to his survival. Yet now, Jupiter found himself waiting curiously to see if she would tell more.

Mary paused for only a moment. She was surprised, not only by how many memories were flooding back to her, but also by how natural it felt to share them with this stranger. She continued on, "I must say that I knew very little about my mother. She was an invalid, or at least it was claimed that she was. Every morning I would be required to attend to my mother's bedside to wish her good health. I hated this duty. It was always my feeling that she wished to be sick and confined to her bed, and I felt very angry about this. When she would speak to me, it would only be to tell me of her suffering. I knew she wanted sympathy, but I felt none. Still, out of duty, I would feign some concern. I doubt that this was adequate for her, but it was all I had to give.

"My father's death seemed to affect her deeply which I thought strange as she rarely saw him. She died within a year of his death. At her funeral, I remember feeling only relief that I no longer had to go to her bedside every day. I know it sounds harsh and cruel of me, but I really knew very little about her and she seemed to know nothing of me.

"After her death, my older brother who was only fourteen at the time, declared himself the head of the household. That was thirteen years ago, and he has ruled our household ever since. It is because of my brother that I am here."

Without thinking about what he was doing, Jupiter began to eat as he listened.

"You see, my brother Charles has banished me here to America. It is his way of punishing me for disobeying him. He had arranged for me to marry my cousin William and I refused to do so. Now before you ask why I did not just marry William," she said, knowing full well that Jupiter would never ask her any such thing, "it is because William is an absolute swine."

Jupiter was surprised by what she said and how she said it. Before he could stop himself, he looked up from his meal and found her looking straight at him. Quickly, he looked back down at his plate.

"Oh, I do not exaggerate Jupiter," Mary said, feeling like she just had to finally say these things out loud to somebody. She was tired of holding in the truth, and now wanted only to speak openly and honestly. "My cousin William is a disgusting and vile human being. He has always been that way. Whenever he would come to visit, my younger sister Ann and I would always hide from him. He was five years older than I and eleven years older than Ann, and he would try to corner us to place his hands under our dresses."

Jupiter stopped eating. It was completely inappropriate for her to be saying these things to him, but how should he handle it? She had crossed a line that would put him in a very difficult position.

Mary noticed that Jupiter was uncomfortable by what she had said. "Oh Jupiter, please do not stop eating. We are both full grown adults who have surely seen enough of the world to understand it. We are also prisoners in a *waterless pit*, who once we leave this place, will never meet again. At least around you, let me not have to follow the suffocating rules of conduct. I am so tired of formalities, politesse and decorum. I want to say the truth and perhaps, here in this wilderness, is a safe place to do so. Perhaps, this will be the most freedom either one of us will ever know. Will you not allow me to speak openly?"

Mary did not wait for any reply from Jupiter, but instead, she once again let loose the thoughts she had held in for so long. "When I was thirteen years old, there was a very sacred ceremony where I took an oath to, with all of my heart, serve God and Truth until the end of my days. And when I took that oath, I did it fully believing in what I was doing. Even though I was still a child, I believed in all of it. Yet, those around me have always demanded that I abide by rules that deplore Truth and love only lies. I am so tired of it Jupiter. I am so tired of watching men like my brother reap death and destruction with their deceitful ways, and claim they do so in the Name of God. I am so tired of being expected to pretend that I do not feel and think the way I truly do. I am so tired of having to keep silent about evil things, when all I want is to scream aloud and reveal the truth for all to hear.

"Somehow when I heard your sweet song, Jupiter, it came clear. Here in this place that was to be my worst punishment, I am determined to find my greatest gift. I have come to the decision that, here, I will abandon my worldly self and work to find and embrace God's Truth, however inconvenient it may be."

Jupiter looked up at Mary's face and saw the pleading question in her eyes. She was asking him to give her one tiny word or gesture of affirmation. Somewhere deep inside, there was a part of him that sincerely wanted to say something, but anything that he could possibly say would put him in a very vulnerable position. He could not trust this strange woman. It would be madness on his part to do so, and he knew that the price for trusting the wrong person could be very high.

Mary sighed at the empty silence. She hoped that he would have been able to see the sincerity that was in her heart, and that would make all the difference. But how could she blame him? His prison had been far worse than the one she knew. She looked at him sadly and said, "Jupiter, I cannot expect you to trust me." Then desperately needing just to be alone, she rose from the table and walked outside.

Jupiter looked at the cold food left on his plate, and then slowly began to pile the dishes onto the tray. She wasn't insane. He knew that now. But why did it now frighten him even more, to know that she was not mad? He wanted to forget everything she had just said the same way he always forgot things that could interfere with his well-ordered existence. But this time, something was different. No matter how hard he tried to push her words away, they would not leave him alone.

Chapter 9

The next morning, when Mary awoke, there were none of the usual feelings of sadness that she had come to expect. Instead, she continued to feel driven by a strange, undefined resolve. She sat up, placed her feet on the floor and walked over to the wash basin. There, she splashed water on her face and in her mind, she said a prayer:

O Lord, our Lord,
Teach me good judgment and knowledge:
For I have believed thy commandments.

Mary took her time in carefully dressing and grooming for the day. She was determined not to succumb to the emptiness that had threatened her before. By putting thought and sincerity in every small task she did, she knew that she was infusing life into those moments. If she was going to find her way to God's Truth, then she would have to thoughtfully pave a solid path in the right direction.

When she was ready, she sat down and waited for Jupiter to arrive with breakfast. Mary wondered what he would be thinking this morning. If he was determined not to sit or speak with her, should she try to convince him otherwise or just accept his decision? She was hopeful that he may have decided to trust her even a little. Even a small amount of trust would make it possible to become friends, and right now she desperately needed a friend.

Mary was still sitting at the table and thinking about what she might say to Jupiter when she heard a soft knock at the door. Her heart beat faster. Was there anything that she could say that would make him not look at her the same way he looked at Pierce and Montford? "Come in Jupiter," she said.

Jupiter came through the door carrying a tray which he placed on the table. Mary was relieved to see that once again he had brought two plates. Without being asked, he then sat down across from her, and silently poured the tea. After the cups were full, he sat back in his chair and said, "My Lady, as I recall, you said that your cousin is a swine." Jupiter still had his usual stone expression, but there was a hint of amusement in his voice.

Mary almost began to weep with happiness. She had been so starved for any genuine act of kindness that she found herself almost overcome with gratitude at such a sincere gesture. Before, she felt completely alone in her silent desolation, and now it appeared that finally someone was offering to hear her voice. She laughed a little and replied, "Yes Jupiter, he is a dirty filthy swine."

She stirred some milk into her cup, and then brought the warm tea to her lips before she continued with her story. "My sister Ann and I became very skilled at hiding when Cousin William came to visit," she said. "However, I felt so sorry for the servant girls who would suffer his attentions. My brother Charles was very fond of William, but only I think, because William would obey his every command. Even Charles could sometimes not help but be disgusted by William who had many repulsive habits." She paused and then added, "Perhaps his most disgusting habit was eating whatever he could pull from his nose."

Jupiter suddenly broke out in laughter almost spilling his tea, but within a few seconds he regained his composure. It had been a very long time since he had laughed out loud and this outburst had caught him off-guard. He quietly sat and worried about the appropriateness of what he had just done.

71

Mary was pleasantly surprised to hear such a deep and hearty laugh. "Oh please Jupiter, feel free to laugh," she said. "It is a perfectly ridiculous situation."

Jupiter smiled slightly, but did not laugh again because the moment had passed. It did surprise him however, that he was feeling free to laugh in this woman's presence, and that he was already looking forward to a time when he might spontaneously laugh like that again. He could not remember the last time he had done that.

Mary then continued on with her story. "Of course, as we both know, sometimes very small children do this until they are taught that it is unacceptable, but William was no small child. Sometimes he would do it in a roomful of people when he thought no one was watching. And this is the man my brother wanted me to marry." She paused to sip some more tea, then looked over at Jupiter who was obviously amused by her story, but for the most part still continued to keep his eyes only on his plate. "In truth though, I now regret that I told my brother I would not marry William," she said sadly.

Jupiter briefly looked up and into her eyes. "Why?" he asked, amazed by the fact that he had just looked at her and asked a question freely.

"After I had refused to be married, Charles made the decision to betroth my sister Ann to William. Ann is only sixteen years old, and she is far more delicate than I. How she could possibly bear a marriage to this animal, I do not know. It is now my regret that I did not take this suffering for her. However, at the time I had no idea that Charles would go this far."

Jupiter could hear the sorrow and helplessness in her voice. It seemed so strange that he should be sitting there and listening to her express her pain. Suddenly, he found himself begin to feel something that he had not felt in a very long time. He began to feel a little sympathy for the woman.

Staring down at her plate, Mary sadly said, "Ann is so very young, and William is so vile. I thought that even Charles would have more compassion for his own sister than that.

Unlike me, Ann had always been good to him. However, I underestimated the extent of his selfishness. He was just so intent to marry one of his sisters to William that he did not care. You see, by marrying Ann to William, Charles not only keeps the family line intact, but he will also ensure that William's wealth stays within the family."

Mary absently traced her finger along the wood grain in the table. She looked up briefly to see Jupiter watching her. At that point, she realized that she had to explain a little more if he was going to fully understand.

"Jupiter, it is not simply about wealth. In my family it is considered very important to keep the bloodline from being broken. My family is part of a large and powerful Royal Family. There are many different branches to it, and it now reaches around the world. In this family, the female line is very important, and some see it as the line that must be continued at all costs. The line from mothers to daughters is sacred, and men who are born of these mothers secure their power by marrying back into the same bloodline. It is then important that his children continue to marry into the same female line. If they are cousins and a man's grandmother is the same as his wife's grandmother, it is often considered a holy match of great potential. Charles believes that marrying one of his sisters to William would create such a holy match, and be pleasing in the eyes of God. It would also increase the chances of producing exceptional children. This is why it was so important to Charles that at least one of his sisters marry William."

Jupiter knew very little about families. He was not sure what to think about the kind she was describing, but he was intrigued by the strangeness of it.

Mary paused only for a second to finish off the now cold tea. "When I discovered my brother's new plan I pleaded with him. I pleaded with him to let Ann be, and I would agree to marry William. His reply was only that it was too late—that I had lost my opportunity to marry Cousin William. Not knowing what else to do, I begged on bended knee, but that only seemed to make him more determined to carry out this plan. Charles saw how much it hurt me, and it pleased him to see me suffer. Even as children, I had always flouted his authority, and he had always threatened to take revenge upon me. I should have seen it coming, Jupiter, but sadly I did not.

"Several days later, it was the middle of the night when I was awakened by servants who told me that Charles had requested to see me right away. They assisted me to get dressed, and I hurried as quickly as I could. I was hoping that Charles had changed his mind about Ann. However, I was not taken to speak with Charles in private. Instead, I was taken to the front door where a coach was waiting. Before I was put inside, Charles arrived smiling that wicked smile I hate so much. He told me that he was sending me into exile, and went on to explain that he will wait for God to tell him when, or even if, I should return to England. Charles enjoyed making it even worse by assuring me that he would give Ann my regrets for being unable to attend her wedding, and that he would also pass on my best wishes to her and Cousin William.

"When I tried again to beg of him not to do this, he simply turned his back on me and walked away. Before I could follow him, two servants took me by my arms and put me into the coach. From there, I was taken to a port and placed aboard a horrid vessel captained by the devil's spawn, and manned by scoundrels of every sort. And now here I am, imprisoned in the wilderness of America—not knowing for how long I will remain here, and full of worry and dread for the welfare of my sister back home."

Mary stopped talking and began to cry. She crossed her arms on the table and buried her head inside of them. Jupiter sat for a moment, not knowing what to do. Finally, he decided that it was likely best to do nothing at all, and just leave her to be on her own. Without a word, he carefully piled everything back on the tray and quietly went outside.

Mary was glad when Jupiter left the cabin. She needed some time to collect her thoughts. Until that moment, the entire ordeal had seemed more like a terrible nightmare then reality. Telling the story aloud made it all too real. She was a prisoner in the wilderness thousands of miles from home, and by now, Ann would certainly be married to William. There was no denying the awful truth.

For a long while, Mary stayed with her head resting on her arms. Eventually, she stood up and walked over to the basin, where she splashed the cool water on her face then wiped it dry with a white cloth. She looked in the mirror, straightened her bonnet and made sure that all of her hair was tucked securely underneath it. There were to be no more tears of abandon. If she was to continue her pursuit of God's Honest Truth, she would have to find the fortitude to keep going forward. Pushing up her sleeves, she went outside to begin her laundry.

Chapter 10

Mary waited impatiently at the table. The late afternoon sun streamed through the wide open door, and Jupiter had yet to arrive. His chores in the barn and garden kept him away from the cabin, so she had not seen him since her tearful breakdown. She was concerned that he may not want to return. After all, they were still strangers and she had poured her heart out to him. There was no doubt that their old predictable relationship was gone forever, and now she didn't quite know what to expect. She only hoped that he would not dislike and avoid her for what might seem like her continuous outbursts.

When Jupiter finally showed up with a tray and plates for two, Mary was surprised by how much seeing him enter the cabin lifted her spirits. She felt even better when he again sat down at the table without waiting to be asked.

"Good day, My Lady," he said. "Shall I pour the tea?

"Please sir," replied Mary cheerfully.

While waiting for him to arrive, she had already considered how their conversation might go. For the moment, she did not want to talk about her own situation in case she would begin to cry again. If she cried for a third time in front of Jupiter, it could make him hesitant to talk with her at all, and she did not want to risk that happening.

She decided that it would be best if she tried to get Jupiter to talk about his own life, and was hoping that he may now feel comfortable enough to do that. As he finished pouring the tea, she thanked him and then asked, "If you do not mind this question, when did you leave the plantation? I am of course referring to the plantation in North Carolina where you grew up."

Jupiter sipped some tea from his cup. He swallowed it back and then was quiet. Mary began to wonder if he would ever answer her. Finally he said, "I was sold from there when I was eight years old."

"And you do not remember anything of a mother or a father?" Mary asked, relieved that he had answered her question.

"No, I had no father or mother. As I said before, there was a slave Martha who took care of me when I was very young. No one ever spoke to me of parents. In all honesty, I cannot remember many families on the plantation. Most of the slaves were on their own. Some of them may once have had families, but they may have been broken up when family members were sold off."

Mary knew about slavery and had always disliked it, but she had never really thought about the vile details involved in its day to day practice. The idea that people could be sold away from their families filled her with disgust. Perhaps Ann had been married off to a beast, but at least she knew where she was and would one day see her again.

"Please, would you tell me more about your life Jupiter?" she asked. "I need to understand what it is like. Tell me everything that you feel comfortable allowing me to know."

Jupiter was not sure how much he should tell her. He certainly had never told anyone about his life before. What was past was past, and there was no point in remembering any of it. At least, this is what he usually told himself. Today, however, he couldn't help feeling a little differently. He wasn't sure why he was feeling this way. Today, he felt like he wanted someone to hear about the things that had happened to him—things that he had tried very hard to forget, but had never been able to shake entirely. For some reason, he felt compelled to say things out loud that had long been locked away inside of his mind.

Despite the fear that cautioned him, he instinctively took a leap of faith, and began to tell her his story. "My earliest memories are of living in the master's house in a room off of the kitchen that I shared with other house slaves. Martha, who took care of me, was the household cook. Although I was too young to remember when I began my service, I am certain that as soon as I was old enough to carry a tray, I started my training as a valet. There was an old slave by the name of Tom who was in charge of my on-going education. He was a very severe teacher, and I learned very quickly to follow his instructions to perfection.

"Mr. Powel was my master. He seemed to take great pride in me, but Mrs. Powel disliked me terribly. Why she felt this way, I do not know, but she would often do things to make my life miserable. When I was busy working and Mr. Powel was not around, she would come up behind me and slap my head for no reason that I know of. I dreaded whenever Mr. Powel had to go away from home for several days and I was left alone with her.

"By the time I was eight years old, I was quite skilled at the tasks of a gentleman's slave, and it was around this time that Mr. Powel decided to sell me. I suppose he felt that I was old enough and skilled enough that I would then fetch a reasonable sum."

Jupiter hesitated for a moment. He could not believe all that he had just said. Could those words really be coming from his mouth? Surely they must be from someone else. He would never dare to be so careless, and reveal so much about himself. What devil had possessed him to tell her the story of his life? After all the years, he had disciplined himself to keep his thoughts safely hidden away inside his own mind; now, here he was foolishly talking without reserve. Yet, he somehow knew he could not stop. Having seen the door wide open, it was impossible for him to close it now.

"This was my worst fear come true," he continued, "as I was terrified of being sold. I remember once seeing slaves being put in the cart to be taken to market. I do not know how old I was when I saw this, but I know that I was very young. So young that it surprises me I can remember it at all. I suppose that this memory was not lost to time because it was so dreadful. It was a horrible thing to hear the crying, and see the sorrow in their faces. I remember clearly the sight of Mr. Powel and his overseer forcing the people into the back of a wagon. I am not sure the exact number, but I remember three of them. There was an old man, a boy and there was also an older girl named Sarah. I suppose that I only remember her name because I believe I recall her playing games and singing songs to me. But the memory is so faint that I am not sure it is real. Regardless, I have never been able to forget Sarah's name or her face. I remember how she looked directly at me as the wagon pulled away. Tears were streaming down her cheeks and even at my young age, I could feel her anguish. She looked at me with such pleading eyes. I have never been able to remove her heart-broken face from my memory even though I have tried." At this point Jupiter went quiet, unable to continue.

Mary was horrified by his story. For a moment, she could not think of anything to say. What could be said about such brutality? Finally, she knew that it was up to her to encourage him to keep speaking. "Please Jupiter, I would like to hear everything," she said, and then waited hopefully for him to continue.

Jupiter was surprised at just how easily and natural the words were now flowing from his mouth. They had not choked him like he suspected they might. Instead, they made him feel like he was beginning to breathe again. Jupiter was not going to stop there. He had to keep going, regardless of the consequences. He had to let her know the whole truth. Somebody should hear the truth and somebody needed to tell it.

"So you can now understand why being sold away was my greatest fear," he said. "It was a terrifying thing to be taken from the only home you knew, even if this home was far from perfect."

Mary understood exactly what he meant.

Jupiter looked only at his hands and continued talking. "So without any warning, my greatest fear became a reality when I was almost nine years old. After attending to Mr. Powel, I returned to the kitchen where Martha suddenly grabbed me in her large arms and hugged me tightly, which was very unlike her. She was quite upset, and was saying things to me that I could not understand. I was very confused by it all, but then she told me that I was to pack my things as Mr. Powel had decided that I should be taken to auction. I was terrified and could not believe it. At first, I refused to pack a thing, but Tom took a riding crop to me, and I realized then that I had no choice.

"As I climbed into the waiting wagon with Mr. Powel, he paid no attention to my constant crying and without saying a word, drove me to a slave market in Richmond. I still have a clear memory of standing on that platform with the auctioneer shouting and so many strange men staring at me. It was not really clear to me what was happening until it was done, and a smiling gentleman took my arm declaring that I was now his property.

"I had been purchased by Mr. Lynch. He was more demanding than Mr. Powel, but at least he did not have a wife that hated me. I worked well and was an obedient slave. The problem came just over two years into my service there.

"During my time at the Lynch plantation, I became good friends with a slave boy named Simon. Simon was about my age and lived in the big house also. His work was to attend to Paul, the son of Mr. Lynch. Paul was also around the same age. Simon's duties were to serve and amuse the boy with games. My own position as a gentleman's slave meant that I was not allowed to play, and I could not help but feel jealous when I would see Simon running, laughing and climbing trees. Of course, it was not always good for Simon as Paul would sometimes get angry and have him whipped. But still, he could play, which is something that was not allowed for me.

"At night Simon and I shared a small room at the back of the house, and that is when we would talk. We would tell each other all kinds of things, and I began to see him as my friend. In the daytime, we would never speak, but at night we would talk until we fell asleep. I had become very attached to Simon, who I began to see like a brother. I was a child with no one else in the world, and Simon took on a great deal of importance in my life.

"I had been with the Lynch family over a year when Simon began to tell stories about a place where slaves could escape and not be found. He said he had heard the story from an old man on a nearby plantation. This place was many days walk, and could only be found when the moon was full and red in color. No white man could ever enter because of a river creature that guarded the land and made a horrible noise to frighten away slave owners who might come looking for runaways. This land had no name because no name could describe its beauty. There were many beautiful gardens filled with fruit, vegetables, deer and rabbit. There was also a friendly Indian tribe that saw it as their duty to welcome and protect escaped slaves.

"Simon and I would talk about this place every evening. We took turns creating stories about how we would runaway together, and live in freedom with our new Indian brothers. Often we would talk about it as though it were real, and I think that sometimes there were moments when we had convinced ourselves that it really existed.

"My life with the Lynch family could be very demanding, and some days were extremely difficult, but I could always look forward to storytelling with Simon. This part of my life kept me feeling hopeful, in spite of all the rest. Then one day, everything changed."

Jupiter picked up his now cold tea. He stared at it as he swirled it in the cup, and then looked over at Mary. When she saw what was in his eyes, she felt a little afraid to hear the rest of the story. Still, she knew that she needed to hear what he had to say. "Please go on," she softly asked of him.

Jupiter sighed and looked back at his teacup. He touched the red rose that was painted on the saucer and continued to speak. "Simon and Paul had begun to have more and more conflicts between them. Paul was getting older and beginning to assert himself as master. He demanded greater obedience from

Simon. Simon was beginning to resent this new relationship, and was not always playing the games as instructed by Paul.

"One day, I was in the garden near the kitchen picking some fresh herbs for the cook, as I was sometimes required to assist her, when I saw Simon and Paul get into a fight. It happened that Simon had found a walnut with an unusual shape. He showed it to Paul telling him that the unusual shape meant that it was magic. Paul, of course, wanted the magic walnut for himself, but Simon refused to hand it over. They argued and then fought. Simon, who was larger and stronger than Paul, came out as the winner. Paul was humiliated, and with his nose dripping blood he went running into the big house.

"It was not long before Mr. Lynch stormed out of the house with the whip in his hand. Simon could see how angry Mr. Lynch was, and must have imagined that he would be whipped to death. He ran behind a tree and began to plead with Mr. Lynch not to whip him. Mr. Lynch had just grabbed him by the arm, and was about to strike him hard when I heard Simon say something I could not believe he would ever say. He began to tell Mr. Lynch that he should whip me instead because I was planning to run off and hide with the Indians.

"For Mr. Lynch, who did not like to lose so much as a single penny, the idea having one of his slaves escape was concerning—that one of his more valuable Negroes would run away, made him very anxious. He forgot about whipping Simon, and instead, began to ask him questions about my plan to run. Simon told him all of our imagined stories as if they were real and even made up more. I just stood nearby not knowing what to do or to say.

"Mr. Lynch came to me and asked me if I had any thoughts to run away. I denied it and told him it was all just stories, but he did not believe me. He had already lost three slaves to escapes and would not risk losing another. It was then that he decided that he would sell me before I could run, but first he wanted to teach me a lesson.

"I heard that he had paid more money for me than what was usually paid for a boy my age, and he knew that I would be worth even more now that I was older and better trained. He did not want to leave any tell-tale whip marks on me because buyers always look for whip marks. They believe it is an indication of a troublesome slave and the value goes down considerably. Mr. Lynch was intent on making a good profit, so he came up with a severe punishment that would not affect my price. Instead of whipping me, he tied me naked to a post in the barn, and made a single cut in my thigh with an ordinary sickle. He thought that, this way, any scar left behind could be said to have been just a work accident.

"Then he ordered Simon to mix salt and cold water together in a bucket and dump it over the wound. For three days, he kept me tied there and each day Simon would come three times and pour the cold salt water on me. I could not believe that Simon would do this to me. He was supposed to be my friend. When he came in the barn, he never said a word or looked me in the eye. He would just come in, pour the saltwater and then go out. I would scream and cry in pain, and beg him to help me, but he still would not even look at me.

"After I was untied, I was taken back to the house again. Mr. Lynch put me in my old room with Simon. The cook was instructed to care for me and see that I heal as quickly as possible. I did not say a word to Simon from that point onward. He tried to speak to me once, but I turned away from him and he never tried again. I learned my lesson well: a slave could have no friends.

"As soon as I was healed and strong again, Mr. Lynch took me to an auction in Williamsburg. There I was purchased by Captain Springsteen, who I have been with ever since and have had no problems to speak of."

Jupiter went silent and looked over at Mary. Tears were streaming down her face. This was a completely new situation, and he did not know what to do. He had not meant to say everything that he had. Should he say something now? Should he get up and leave as he did the other night? Before he could decide what to do, she lunged forward and grabbed his hand in hers.

"Oh Jupiter, I knew that slavery was terrible, but to hear it from your lips and see it in your eyes, I am only beginning to understand. How could a human being with a soul do that to a little boy? Please, if you are to know just one thing this day, you must know that I am not like Simon. I pledge to you now before God that you are my friend, and I will never forsake you. That is my sacred promise and, as long as I live, it will never be broken."

Jupiter looked into her eyes, and then at her hand that seemed to burn into his. He wanted to pull away from this fire, but it was as though an unseen force held him in place. Questions were racing through his mind. Why did she pledge her friendship? What did she want from him? How could he have carelessly told her the secrets of his past? He let his guard down, and as a result, was now in an impossible situation with no idea what to do next.

Jupiter suddenly felt dizzy and off balance. He was afraid to try and stand, yet afraid to stay sitting in a chair that seemed to be dissolving beneath him. The only thing there was to keep him from falling was something that frightened him so badly he wished it would just go away. The only thing stopping him from sliding off of the edge of the world was the touch of a woman's hand.

Chapter 11

The next morning Mary found herself waking with an entirely new perspective. For the first time since she had left England, she was not feeling like she was in as strange place. As she lay in her bed and looked around the room, the grey walls of the cabin did not look as sad and impoverished as they had before. Instead, there was strange beauty in the flowing lines of the wood, and a sweet security within the impressive solid craftsmanship.

Listening to Jupiter's story the night before had somehow changed things. Mary wasn't sure how it had happened, but only knew that it did. She surprised even herself when she suddenly made a pledge before God to this man who she still knew so little about. According to the code of The Vine, her pledges were unbreakable. The only other person she had ever pledged to before was her sister Ann. When their mother died, she had promised her baby sister that she would never leave her alone. How could she have known that her own brother would ultimately break this sacred pledge for her?

As she washed and dressed, her thoughts were of Jupiter. She was still a little worried that something may destroy the trust he had begun to feel for her, and that he may just stop speaking entirely. After enjoying some reprieve from her empty exile, she did not think she could bear it if the silence returned. She wanted desperately for Jupiter to talk with her again. But why should this man who had suffered so much trust her?

Surely he must see her as just another one of the people who keep him imprisoned in slavery? How could she be any different in his eyes?

When Jupiter arrived with breakfast, Mary was elated to see him softly smile at her as he set the tray on the table. This was a good sign. He was not having second thoughts about their new relationship. He would still continue to speak with her.

"Did you sleep well My Lady?" he asked, as he set out the plates.

"Yes, thank you Sir, I did," she happily replied.

Jupiter sat in the chair across from her and said, "That is good." He poured the tea and casually mentioned, "The weather has been excellent this summer. The crops in the garden are doing very well."

As he buttered his bread, Jupiter could not help but feel as though he were in a dream. How is it that he could just walk in here and speak with her like this? Surely he would wake up soon.

Mary felt as though she had just awakened from a nightmare. The desolation and loneliness had faded away with her new consciousness. Now she had a friend with whom she could talk honestly. There were so many questions she wanted to ask Jupiter, but did not know where to begin. Although he had already told her a great deal, she still wanted to know more. Mary wanted to know everything there was to know about this man and his life. Before she could think it through, she suddenly blurted out one of the questions in her mind. "Do you know why your mother would name you Jupiter?" she asked.

Jupiter was surprised by the question. He had never really thought much about his name at all, but he knew for certain it did not come from his mother. "It is the slave owners who name the slaves," he replied, taking a sip of tea.

"I was just curious," said Mary, "as Jupiter is such an unusual name."

"Is it?" he asked, trying to think if he had come across any other slave by the same name. He did not know too much about it, but knew that it was exclusively a slave name.

"Yes, it is very unusual," Mary took a bite of bread. "Do you know the stories of Jupiter?"

"Other than myself, I do not know any Jupiter. What stories do you speak of?" he asked curiously.

Mary suddenly realized that despite his good manners and fine speech, he had not been educated in any formal subjects. She felt a little foolish that she had not considered this before raising the subject. "The name comes from Roman mythology," she said. "Jupiter was the name of a Roman god." She could see that Jupiter looked both amazed and confused by what she had just told him. If he were to understand fully, she would have to explain more. "Long ago," she said, "before the England and America we know, there was a great empire of people called Romans. The Romans lived across the sea at a time when America was still only populated by Indians."

Jupiter had known that at one time the Natives were the only people in America, and that the white men came from across the sea, but he hadn't given any of it much thought. He only knew this much because of a few things he picked up when accompanying Springsteen to various Native villages. Stories of the past were never of much interest to him before, but this morning he was beginning to sense that the past may be more important than he ever imagined.

Mary continued to explain, "The Romans had an enormous empire. It was established by the force of a great and powerful army. They would march into the bordering lands and violently take control of them. It was their belief that they were superior among men. Because of this, they thought that they had the right to take what belonged to others and to enslave the people whom they had conquered. They were ruthless, brutal and they controlled the people through fear and shame. They also happened to follow a very complex religion. It was an old religion that actually went back to a time before the Roman Empire, and involved the worship of many gods. One of those gods was named Jupiter."

Jupiter began to laugh out loud. All his life he had been told that as a slave, he was less than a human being, and now it turns out that they named him after a god. "They would name their slave after a god!" he said as he laughed.

Mary smiled widely. She was delighted that she had once again made him laugh. "Oh Sir," she humorously added, "not just any god. You are named after the god of gods. Jupiter was the almighty king of heaven!"

Jupiter laughed even louder and Mary, now fully infected, began to laugh out loud too. It had been such a long time since she had laughed. Her spirit soared to feel it again. This was more than sharing a joke. This was about receiving a very precious gift.

For Jupiter, he could not remember ever laughing this hard in his life. He bellowed so loud he feared that he could be heard miles away. The crazed joy poured out of them both, and their eyes were blinded with tears.

As their laughter finally subsided, Jupiter looked directly at Mary who looked back at him. He spoke in an earnest voice and said, "Until this day I have never thought once about the name I was given. Thank you for telling me this."

Mary smiled. Although she had thanked him many times, it was the first time that Jupiter had ever said 'thank you' to her. To pay her this small but genuine honour, made her know that his eyes were beginning to open. He was beginning to see her as a real person, and not just a burden to be resented.

Mary thought of something else she should tell Jupiter. She looked into his eyes that still sparkled from the tears and said, "There is also another Jupiter, and as long as there are no clouds to hide him, he shows himself every night in the sky. He is a bright star in the heavens."

Jupiter looked at her in amazement. How many nights had he found comfort by gazing into the star-filled sky? Whenever life was just too much to bear, he could always count on that magnificent constant. When he felt too weak and broken, he could always look up from the dark earth to the magic above it, and would feel whole and strong again. To think that every time he had done this, there had always been a star up there with his name.

Mary set down her teacup and said, "Tonight after it gets dark enough, and if the night is clear, I will show you the star that is Jupiter."

Jupiter felt like he could not wait for evening to come. The breakfast was now done and he was filled with a new energy that made him want to move. "Well for now," he chuckled, getting up from his chair, "the king of heaven must feed the chickens if we are going to have eggs for tomorrow."

Mary laughed as she watched him gather up the plates and place them on the tray. She desired him to stay longer, but was cautious about making Jupiter feel pressured. The last thing she wanted was for him to abandon her and return to his silence.

Later that evening, when the sky was dark enough to see the brightest stars, Mary went out on the porch and called to Jupiter. From near his shack, he was already looking at the sky, and hoping that she would remember. He still did not feel comfortable approaching her without first being asked.

Jupiter hurried over to where she was, and they stood in front of the cabin side by side looking up at the sky. "If you look directly above the tallest pine tree there," Mary pointed to her left, "just straight above it. Do you see the brightest star in that area? That is Jupiter."

He looked in the place that Mary had indicated, and Jupiter could not only see the brightest star that was just above the tallest pine, but he realized that he knew that star well. He was amazed that not only was it one of the brightest in the sky, but it was also one that was very familiar to him.

"I know that star," he said. "But all the times I have looked at it, I have never dreamed that it was named Jupiter—like me." As he stared at the beautiful star, he felt warm throughout his body. The peacefulness he always felt from looking at the night's sky now had a new and wondrous dimension.

That evening Jupiter decided to make a bed outside his shack on some soft nearby grass. There, he fell asleep while looking at his star.

Chapter 12

The next few days, Mary and Jupiter became more comfortable with each other as their friendship grew. They began to work together in completing many of the chores. Mary, who in the very beginning felt depressed by the work, was now happily learning all of the ordinary skills needed to live without servants. She still, however, left most of the meal preparation to Jupiter. After she had tried her hand at making supper one evening, they both concluded that, for now, it was best to leave that job to him.

In the evenings, Jupiter would often entertain them both with singing. Sometimes he would sing songs he had heard before, and sometimes he would create entirely new ones. For the first time in his life, he was finding joy in sharing his music with another person.

Mary would help them pass the time by retelling all of the stories she knew which included many fairy tales from her childhood. She also taught Jupiter everything she could remember from her history and geography lessons.

When Mary discovered that Jupiter could read, she was delighted. As a child, he had secretly picked it up, and then later on was encouraged by Springsteen to improve the skill. However, Springsteen never allowed him to read literature or educational materials of any sort. His reading was restricted to papers pertaining to business and legal affairs. Springsteen was not strong when it came to deciphering contracts and calculating sums, and had come to depend on Jupiter to assist him with various documents. This was of course a secret kept between them.

Mary wished that she had all of her books to give to Jupiter, but the only book she had was her Bible. She offered it to him, and he gladly took it. He had known that this was considered a very important book, and was eager to see for himself what was in it.

One afternoon, Mary had just finished tidying the cabin when she decided to find Jupiter to have one of their discussions that she enjoyed so much. She found him sitting under a tree and reading the Bible. She could see that he was already about half-way through the Old Testament.

"Good day Jupiter. May I sit beside you?" she asked.

Jupiter was happy to see her smiling face especially since he was in the middle of reading The Book of Job. It was nice to be awakened from that dark dream. "Please My Lady," he said, "do sit down."

Mary sat down beside him and asked, "So what is your opinion of the book so far?"

Jupiter smiled at her. Although he found the book far from dull, it was very confusing. Hoping that his words would not upset Mary, but trying to be honest he said, "Well there are many interesting stories, but I am perplexed as to why there is so much killing and relations between men and women. I did not expect this for a book that is considered very holy."

Mary laughed, "Well the Bible is not usually described in that way, but yes, I suppose those two elements are prominent themes. Perhaps, it is because that is how our world was, and still is for that matter. For me, the book's value is in finding the special and sometimes hidden messages within the pages."

Jupiter thought that anyone would certainly have to look for deeper meanings if that strange collection of stories was going to make any sense at all. A lot of what he read seemed terribly depressing.

As Mary thought about Jupiter's reaction, it suddenly occurred to her that she did not know what sort of religious education he might have been given. "Have you ever attended church?" she asked.

Jupiter looked at her and laughed slightly, "I have stood outside several times whenever Captain Springsteen felt pressure to attend, but slaves are not allowed inside. However, I have heard the words of Reverend Ward."

"And who is Reverend Ward?" asked Mary.

"Reverend Ward," said Jupiter "was hired by slave owners to come to their plantations and preach to their slaves. Captain Springsteen sent me twice to listen to what he had to say. A barn was our church. We were made to sit on the filthy floor while Reverend Ward stood and preached in front of us. The preaching was always done at night so that it did not interfere with our work in the day. I recall how the light from the lanterns cast a horrible glow and deepened the ugly lines of that man's face. He certainly looked far more like a devil than like a man of God."

Jupiter had not thought about those sermons in a long time. He was aware that the Reverend was still working the plantation circuit, but Springsteen had not made him go to one of those meetings in years.

"The Reverend was the kind of man who loved to have people hear him speak," Jupiter told Mary. "The louder he could make his voice, the more satisfied he was. He would always begin his sermon by proclaiming that he was chosen by God to speak to the Negroes, and had a special message only for our ears. After that, he would shout about Ham who he said was the father of all Negroes. He told us that Ham had committed a great sin, and so, was cursed by God. The curse was that the children of Ham were to live as slaves. Whenever he came to that part of his story, he would shout it so loud and furious that it frightened all of the children and most of the adults."

Mary shook her head in disgust. The lies of men were bad enough, but when they claim to do it in the name of God—

that is an abomination. "He was an evil liar," she exclaimed in anger.

Jupiter was surprised by her passionate response, and suddenly realized that he too was feeling angry. "At the time, I knew that this man was not speaking the truth," he said. "I knew that he was only saying these things to make obedient and fearful slaves, but I could do nothing other than sit quietly on the ground and watch some of the others believe that nonsense." He then looked at Mary and added, "Although I would not have believed his words no matter what, now that you have given me the real story to read for myself, I see what an utter and complete liar he truly was."

"Yes," said Mary, "the story has nothing at all to do with your slavery. Sadly it is not uncommon for the people of my culture to assign meanings to the stories in the Bible to justify their sins. Slavery is certainly a very serious sin."

Jupiter looked at her and smiled. This was the third time she had spoken out so passionately against slavery. He then leaned toward her and said, "However, I must make a confession to you."

Mary wondered what he could mean and was eager for him to explain.

"Since reading the real story of Ham," he continued, "I must confess to you that I did prefer Ham over his brothers. I suspect that usually people do not read it in that way, but for me it was only Ham who saw the truth of his drunken and naked father. He was not afraid to know the truth no matter how painful. His brothers, on the other hand, were fearful and that fear made them look away. They then covered it over and pretended that it was not so. Ham accepts the truth and suffers for it, while his brothers are rewarded for willfully staying subservient, ignorant and blind."

Mary was amazed at what he had just told her. She sighed and said, "I must also confess that I too have always secretly preferred Ham over Shem, however, I have never told anyone this. Those who provided me with my religious training would be horrified to hear me say such a thing."

Although she had been required to engage in many conversations regarding religion and the Bible, Mary had always been very restricted as to the kinds of things she could say. It was such a rare and precious luxury to be able to speak openly and honestly about her thoughts. She leaned her head against the tree, closed her eyes and jokingly said, "Perhaps Jupiter, we see it this way because, in truth, we are the lost children of Ham—you and I—Canaanite slaves imprisoned in the wilderness."

Jupiter smiled and replied, "Then we shall certainly have to find a way to break our wretched curse and escape our wicked cousins Shem and Japheth." This made them laugh together.

The sun was high, and Mary had just finished hanging out the last white sheet to dry. She looked at the row of white fabric and thought how beautiful it looked. The wind suddenly picked up, and the sheets began to flutter. Mary could almost hear the secret music that made them dance. She slowly began to move her feet and dance with them.

Jupiter had just finished dumping out the wash tub when he looked over and saw Mary dancing with the sheets. He laughed and turned the tub completely upside down. His hands began to hit the bottom drumming out a slow methodic rhythm.

Without stopping, Mary looked over at him and smiled. Her body moved to the music of his drum. She raised her arms and twirled about. Her feet hit harder into the earth. The sheets rose up higher on the wind, and flapped freely like the wings of birds.

Jupiter's drumming then began to change. It became faster and took on a new and more complicated rhythm. Mary did not hesitate to move with the new beat. She danced beyond the fluttering of the sheets and out into the openness of the yard. There she continued to whirl about. Her feet were rising and falling against the solid ground, her hands reaching upward as if to catch hold of the sky.

As she began to tire, her dancing gradually slowed and Jupiter's drumming followed suit. She then softly dropped her body down into a thick patch of clover.

Jupiter stopped drumming and went over to her. Mary was lying on her back and smiling. She looked up at him and said, "Do you see it Jupiter? Do you see that magnificent sky? Sit down next to me, and just look at it."

He sat down beside her and looked up. "Have you ever seen such a lovely shade of blue? Have you ever seen the clouds look so fresh and pure?"

Jupiter stared up at the sky. She was right. It was different today. It was more beautiful than he had ever noticed before. He looked back down at Mary who was looking up and smiling at him. Quickly he turned his gaze back toward the sky.

"It is beautiful, My Lady," he quietly said.

Mary stared back up at the sky and sighed. "Are you hungry?" she asked. "I am very hungry."

"Yes," replied Jupiter, "I suppose I am. Shall I go prepare us a midday meal?"

"If you could be so kind, that would be wonderful," answered Mary.

Jupiter got up from the ground and offered his hand to Mary. "Thank you," she said respectfully, "but I believe I shall remain here just a little longer."

"Very well My Lady," he said, and then walked off towards the shack.

Mary continued to look at the sky. She plucked a clover from beside her and held the green up against the blue. Yes, it was true, and it was not just the sky. Everything had become more beautiful.

Chapter 13

The next few weeks, Jupiter and Mary continued to enjoy a life neither had ever imagined possible. Every day, they delighted in a sense of freedom that was completely new to them, and yet somehow, more familiar than anything they had ever known before. What once was their prison, had now become a place of liberty. There were times when it seemed as if the outside world had disappeared entirely, and they would be forever left to their peaceful existence. However, it was inevitable that each day, no matter how wonderful, was a day closer to Samuel Montford's return.

The night before Montford was to arrive, Mary and Jupiter made a commitment to each other that they would keep their new relationship a complete secret. They would go about their business in the same way as would be expected. If anyone were to find out about their friendship, they knew that they would certainly be separated, and Jupiter would be severely punished.

They missed not being able to enjoy their breakfast together, but thought it best if they began the day in their respective roles. That way, they would be comfortably in character when Mr. Montford arrived, and less likely to make any mistake that could raise suspicion.

Samuel Montford arrived shortly after Mary had finished her midday meal. He was alone. This time he had slyly arranged for James Pierce to be too busy sorting out tobacco shipment problems to make the trip.

Mary was feeling both relieved and annoyed. She was relieved that Mr. Pierce had not come along as she found him so distasteful, but she was also annoyed that she would now have to spend the afternoon alone with Mr. Montford. She was not looking forward to having to feign interest in his advances, and would have to put on a convincing performance if the secret plan she had in mind was going to work.

Jupiter began unloading the wagon. He could not help but look when Montford offered his arm to Mary, and then walked with her to the chairs and table that were set out in the shade. The entire scene seemed so unreal. It felt like a strange dream as he watched Mary sit down with that man under the tree. It was not quite clear to him what these feelings were about, but he knew with certainty that maintaining his role of slave would not be as easy as it once was.

Mr. Montford smiled from across the table and asked, "So My Lady, have you been well these past weeks?"

Mary smiled warmly at the man. How many times had she played this part before? The courts of England were all about masquerade. Despite her conviction to live in truth she would have to play the game again. She could return to living honestly after Montford left, but for now she must put on a grand performance.

"Mr. Montford," she began, "in body I have been very well, however, in spirit—that is another matter."

"My dear Lady Mary," responded Montford, "let me say that anything you suffer, I suffer as well. Knowing that you are out here, alone, fills me with pain every day. If there were any way to change your situation, please believe me, I would."

Hiding her real thoughts, Mary smiled and said, "I know that you are a good man Mr. Montford, and it is not your fault that I am here. Sometimes, I just wish I had a way to ease the anguish of loneliness." She placed her hand delicately on the table directly across from where Mr. Montford's hand rested.

Samuel Montford, believing this was his chance, reached forward and placed his hand gently over hers, "Oh Lady Mary, if it were my decision, you would not suffer like this. I truly wish that I could provide you with good company every day, and ease the distress of your solitude."

Mary looked at his eyes and saw his bold ambition. She then quickly looked down, so as not to reveal her repulsion.

Montford grinned at the thought that this woman was succumbing to his charms. Over the years he had become quite adept at seduction. This would be his greatest conquest of all. In the past three weeks, he had thought a great deal about the entire situation, and had recently come to the conclusion that a place within The Holy Family was definitely within his grasp. Things were coming together for him like never before. On top of everything, the war had been all but won, and once victory was official, it would mean that all of his debts would be officially cleared as well. This would put him in a much more powerful position.

Suddenly, Jupiter was standing over them with a tray of tea and biscuits. Mary abruptly removed her hand from under Mr. Montford's. Without a word, he set the tray down on the table and turned to go.

As he walked away, Jupiter thought of how Mary's hand was under Montford's. What did it mean? Was that small gesture part of an act, or was she really enjoying it? She never took her eyes off Montford. She never looked up at him for even a brief second as he set down the tray. It was well known that Montford was highly skilled at charming women. Had he been so foolish to think that Mary would be different from other women in the company of such a man?

Jupiter felt his stomach tighten. That morning, he had been so sure that Mary's friendship was sincere. For weeks, he had trusted her and talked openly. He had even laughed in her presence. Could she have been tricking him? Would she now tell Montford about their every conversation?

Jupiter returned to his shack where he took off his coat and sat down on his cot. He had done something he had once promised himself he would never do. He had revealed himself, and to make it even worse, he had revealed himself to a woman whom he should have known better than to trust.

To try and take his mind off his worries, Jupiter picked up the Bible and began to read where he had previously left off:

And he saith unto them, Why are ye fearful, O ye of little faith? Then he arose, and rebuked the winds and the sea; and there was a great calm.

Jupiter tried to concentrate on the words in front of him, and not to think about what may be happening outside. He continued to read, but struggled to absorb the meaning. Many times, he found himself getting lost on the pages and reading the same passages over again. Finally, after about an hour's time, his anxiety could no longer be suppressed, and he set down the book. Whatever was going to happen, it was still important that he try to maintain order as the dutiful slave. Whatever she was to say or do, he still had to try and ensure his own survival.

Jupiter straightened his cravat, put on his coat and went outside with the intention of collecting the tea things. As he looked from the doorway, he could see Montford lean over the table and put his mouth to Mary's ear. Mary put her hand to her lips and seemed to laugh. Jupiter's heart sank. He braced himself for whatever was to come and walked towards them.

When Jupiter arrived with the tea, Mary intentionally removed her hand from underneath Montford's, hoping that he would see this secret message of her friendship. Because she was so afraid of raising suspicion, she purposely kept her eyes only on Samuel Montford—never even glancing Jupiter's way. She was worried that if she should look at Jupiter, her face may betray her and reveal the truth. Mary had to be very cautious and maintain the charade. This was especially true if she was going to get Montford to divulge the information that she suspected he might have.

After Jupiter had left, Montford smiled at Mary and said, "I have word from your brother the Duke. Now before you ask, I am sad to say that he has not said anything about when you might return to England." He tried not to show his delight that her exile had no end in sight. "But, I do have joyous news for you. Your sister Ann and cousin Lord William have been wed."

Mary felt sick. She needed to cry, but there was Montford sitting across from her smiling and waiting for her happy response. "That is remarkable news!" she said, just barely holding a smile in place. "If only I could have been there to stand with my dear sister on that unforgettable day."

She then decided that she must quickly change the topic to other things; otherwise she was unsure if she would be able to hold back her true feelings. "Mr. Montford, if I may, I would just like to thank you sincerely, for making my stay here more comfortable with all of the fine things you have provided— including an exceptional slave," she said, wanting to steer the topic of conversation towards Jupiter.

"So, there have been no problems with the Negro?" asked Montford, who was confident from what he could see that all was going very well.

"The slave is far more efficient and agreeable than any servant I have ever had in England," replied Mary.

Montford smiled in satisfaction. Even though it was Springsteen who would get the money, he would get the credit for executing the Duke's difficult orders, and often credit was far more valuable in the long run. "When I received news of your arrival, My Lady, I knew that you should have only the finest, and Jupiter is the finest bred Negro. He is dutiful beyond measure, and I went to great lengths to ensure that you should have him. Captain Springsteen, at first, did not want to part with him for any payment, but I was able to persuade him, as I knew that you must have the best of everything."

"Mr. Montford," Mary said as warmly as she could, "I have a very curious nature and was wondering about the slave's origins? Do you know where exactly he came from? Do you know who his parents were?"

Montford chuckled. "How is it that women are always so curious about the strangest things? The story is of a delicate nature, My Lady, and I am not sure if it would be wise for you to hear it." He sat back in his chair and admired how a strand of her hair had fallen from beneath her bonnet. As he stared at it, he thought about how pleasing the memory of this image would be later on, when he was alone.

"Oh Mr. Montford," she said coyly. "Although I am young, I am very well read, and know the facts of this world. Please, I beg of you—you must tell me now that I am even more curious than before." Mary was hoping that she would not have to go to greater lengths to get him to divulge what he knew.

For Montford, her pleading was satisfying enough that he did not think to hold out for more. "Well," he said, "I suppose I could tell you that he was born on the plantation of a Mr. Powel in North Carolina."

Mary was disappointed to only hear what she already knew. She had been hoping that he would tell more than that. "And who were his parents? Do you know anything about them?" she asked.

"Why yes, My Lady," he said, unsure about how much he should divulge to her. There was an unwritten code about what could be said about such things and to whom. Certainly, it wasn't considered a good idea to ever share such information with a woman. Still this was not just any woman. This was a woman from the center branch of The Vine—a very important position that was in sight of becoming his own.

Mary desperately wanted him to say more, but was met with only silence. "Please dear Mr. Montford, please do go on," she pleaded impatiently.

"Well," Montford said, with some hesitance, "his mother was a slave who worked on the plantation and his father—well, he was just a somewhat young and impulsive man at the time. He was a guest at the plantation."

Mary was surprised by what she had just heard and asked, "What do you mean that he was a guest? Are you telling me that Jupiter's father was a white man?"

Montford lowered his voice, which was ludicrous as there was no one else around. "Yes Lady Mary, but I really should not be discussing this kind of a thing with you. It is not proper."

Mary knew that she must get him to say more. She also knew that even if a gentleman protested at first, there was nothing he enjoyed more than an improper conversation with a lady.

"Mr. Montford," she said, placing her hand delicately upon his arm that rested on the table, "I have read a great many books in my life. Some of them had such topics that would cause even a worldly gentleman, such as yourself, to blush. Anything you have to say, I assure you, I am quite capable of hearing." She gracefully withdrew her hand, hoping that this would make him want to draw her back in by revealing more information.

Montford had felt the warm touch of her hand through the sleeve of his coat. He shifted in his chair, and under the table discreetly adjusted his breeches with his free hand. "Well," he said, thinking that this afternoon would be even more pleasant than he imagined, "Jupiter's father is a white man. Like I said, he was a young man at the time, and also a summertime guest at the plantation. The Powel family had two young men around the same age. It was told to me that the young Powel men would often spend evenings in the slave shacks. It is not unusual for men of that age to…..well…."

"Please continue," said Mary, growing impatient. "We are good friends Mr. Montford and you need not feel embarrassed to be truthful with me."

"Yes of course My Lady," said Montford, still a little worried that what he had to say would offend her, but also driven by the desire to say improper things to her. "The young men go there to gain experience of an earthly nature."

Mary kept a smile on her face even though she felt complete disgust. Wanting to encourage Montford to tell her all that he knew, she began to run her fingers along the strand of hair that had fallen from her bonnet.

Montford seeing how she was still smiling, and how she stroked her hair, felt bolstered with enthusiasm. He then happily continued on with the story, "While the young man was visiting, the Powel fellows invited him to the shacks one evening. Being a curious and healthy young man, of course he went with them. Apparently, he became particularly taken by a young slave girl by the name of....let me think....I know it was a Biblical name...oh yes, I remember now. It was Sarah."

When Mary heard the name, she felt so excited that she just wanted to jump up and run to Jupiter. Instead, she kept her mask firmly in place and remained sitting. She must not give even the slightest hint to Montford that she had heard of Sarah before.

Pleased that she seemed so receptive to the unsavory information he had just divulged, Montford was happy to tell her more and added, "After the young man had returned home, it was discovered that Sarah was with-child."

"What did Mr. Powel do when he learned of this? Was he angry?" asked Mary, unsure of just how things worked in America.

Montford laughed and replied, "Oh My Lady, what reason would he have to be angry? His young visitor had just helped to increase Mr. Powel's personal wealth. A healthy male slave is worth money as it is, but with a father from an honourable family, he is of an even higher value. Mr. Powel, I am sure, was very thankful to his visitor."

Mary wanted to scream at Montford and tell him everything that was going through her mind, but instead she kept up her appearance of quiet interest. "Did the young man know he had a son?" she calmly asked.

Montford looked again at the strand of hair that had moved lower and now rested close to Mary's breast. He was pleased to learn that she was not timid about subjects of the flesh. She would make a fine wife in all respects. "Word gets around quickly in American society," he replied, "and the young man did eventually learn about what had happened."

"And how did he feel about it?" asked Mary.

Once again Montford laughed at her naiveté and said, "I suppose, My Lady, that he did not think too much about it at all. This was not in any way an unusual situation. Why, I have heard it said on more than one occasion that the finest blood in America flows through the slave markets."

Now that she had Montford very relaxed and speaking freely, Mary was ready to ask for the final piece to the puzzle. As he had not volunteered the information so far, she knew that he would not give it up easily. With determination she smiled sweetly, leaned toward him and asked, "Dear Mr. Montford, what was the name of this young man who was the father of Jupiter?"

"Oh My Lady, I cannot say," he nervously replied. "Why he is a man of great importance to our United States of America, and it would be very wrong of me to reveal his identity."

Mary was not going to be easily shut out. No matter what it took, she needed to find the name for Jupiter. Leaning farther forward in her chair and reaching out her hand once more to touch him, she said, "But Mr. Montford, I have come to view us as very dear friends. I would be deeply disappointed if you felt that you could not trust me. Do you not feel towards me as I feel towards you?" She was certain that his ambition to win her over would be more powerful than his discretion and male loyalty.

Montford was elated. Was she already close to professing her love for him? His charms seemed to be working even faster than he imagined. "Oh Lady Mary, of course I feel deeply towards you as my dearest friend. It is just that it is unacceptable to reveal the man's name. It is just not done in America." Montford knew he was lying to her. Such information was often shared among reputable businessmen in American high society. It was just not shared outside of that circle.

Mary pulled back in her chair. "Mr. Montford," she said, "you say that you are my true friend, but you do not trust me. I believed that we were close and well—getting closer. Why do you not give me this one small token I ask for?"

Montford now was growing concerned by her tone. She seemed honestly hurt by his reluctance to tell her the name. With only being allowed to visit once a month, there was not much time to woo her. He could not risk losing her interest. Perhaps if he were to reveal a little more without actually divulging the name, this would be enough to satisfy her curiosity. He reluctantly said, "My Lady, I can tell you that his name is on The Declaration of Independence, and that he ranks very high in the Brotherhood."

Knowing that he was now close to breaking, Mary continued to lean forward and took his hand in both of hers. "Oh my dear friend, who will I tell out here?" she said, looking straight into his eyes, "The birds and the rabbits are my only companions. In my terrible exile, you, dear-dear Mr. Montford, are all that I have. Do you not care enough for me to share this small thing? It is merely a name and nothing more. But the fact that you wish to keep this from me leaves me feeling that your friendship is not as true as mine. If it is your desire, then please bind me to secrecy, but do not keep this from me. If you tell me, this will be a secret shared between us forever." She could see in his face that he was beginning to weaken. All he needed was a final temptation that he could not resist. "And if you wish, you may come close and whisper it here," she said, gently tilting her head and offering him her ear.

At first, Montford said nothing and she was afraid that her trick was not going to work. Then suddenly without warning, he jumped to his feet and leaned over the table towards her. She felt his hand on her shoulder pulling her towards him, and then his lips on her ear. He did not say anything for what seemed like the longest time and Mary was annoyed at him for taking such liberties. Yet, she knew she must be patient if she were to learn the name. Finally, in a deep throaty voice he whispered the name into her ear. Mary was surprised as the name was not unfamiliar to her. She had overheard her brother mention it many times before.

As Jupiter approached the table, Montford sat back in his chair and grinned. Mary just looked at Montford and smiled warmly. She did not glance at Jupiter as he stacked up the tea dishes onto the tray.

Montford was feeling very satisfied, but also desirous of further conquest. He decided that he would try to prolong his visit. Feeling now certain that he had won the woman over, and it was only a matter of time before he could have her completely, he confidently asked, "Lady Mary, shall we walk? America is a beautiful place and I doubt that you have had the opportunity to see the magnificent river that is just through those woods."

Mary did not want to walk with Samuel Montford. She just wanted to feign fatigue and be rid of him, but she knew she could not lose an opportunity to get him to tell her everything he might know about Jupiter. "Dear Sir," she said, "I would be delighted to walk with you."

Montford eagerly got up from his chair and then helped Mary from hers. As he offered her his arm, he bluntly ordered Jupiter to return the table and chairs to the cabin.

Jupiter found himself resenting Montford's tone, and couldn't help but imagine picking up one of the chairs and throwing it straight at the man. He was surprised by these feelings of anger. He had always kept such emotions in check, as he knew well, the fate of those who were unable to do this. Picking up the tray from the table, he watched as Montford and Mary walked off arm in arm towards the woods. Now he felt not only anger, but a fool's shame for the blind trust he had put in that woman. He took one of the teacups from the tray and dropped it onto a flat rock that was embedded in the ground.

The cup broke into three pieces, but the single red rose painted on the inside remained intact. Jupiter looked briefly at the broken china and then with the tray in hand, turned and walked away.

Chapter 14

While Mr. Montford and Mary were walking by the river, Jupiter returned the chairs and table to the cabin. He returned to clean up the broken teacup, but decided not to mention it as there were still plenty of other cups and it would not be missed. As he began the supper preparations in his kitchen, he heard Montford call to him to bring the wagon around.

Jupiter was relieved that Montford would finally be leaving. It did not take him long to hitch up the horses and bring the wagon to the front of the cabin. As he obediently held the reigns in wait, he could see out of the corner of his eye that Montford had taken both of Mary's hands in his and then kissed them twice. Mary seemed to respond warmly to his attentions.

As Montford's wagon moved down the road, Jupiter turned without a word and went straight to his shack. He was hoping that Mary would call for him, but he did not hear her voice. He was beginning to feel even more certain that she had indeed been swayed by Montford. Not seeing any other choice in the matter, he decided it would be best if he concentrated on preparing supper, and try not to think about all that had happened.

When the meal was ready, Jupiter hesitated to prepare a plate for himself. If she had been charmed by Montford, then she would certainly no longer want to eat with him. Even though he was full of doubts, he loaded up the tray with a supper for two and headed for the cabin. As he approached, he could see that the door was wide open.

When he walked in, he noticed right away that there was a pottery jug full of colorful wildflowers in the center of the table. He then looked over at Mary, who was standing near the fireplace. She smiled warmly at him.

Jupiter could see that she had changed into a much nicer dress and bonnet. His distrust immediately disappeared, and he was reassured that she was indeed still his friend. Although he felt relief, he was now also feeling foolish and guilty for having doubted her.

"Oh Jupiter," she sighed, "it has been such a tiring afternoon. The hours seemed to drag on forever, and at times I felt like I could no longer pretend." She sat down at the table and looked sadly at him. "When Mr. Montford told me that my poor little sister had been married to William, I thought I might just lose control and scream. However, I kept my true feelings hidden, and summoned up all of my strength to feign happiness."

Jupiter put the tray on the table and sat opposite her. Her face was partially hidden by the jug of flowers. He pushed it to one side and saw the tears in her eyes. "I am sorry My Lady. I know that you love you sister," he said, hoping that his words would help.

Mary looked over at Jupiter and smiled. "If you want to make me feel better, I ask just one thing of you."

"My Lady, anything that will help you, I am willing to do," he said sincerely.

"Please then, no longer call me 'My Lady' or even 'Lady Mary.' Besides Ann who is so far away, you are my only real friend in the world. I want you to call me only Mary. Since you are just Jupiter, I shall be just Mary." She waited to hear him say it.

Jupiter was surprised by her request. He was even more surprised when without a second thought he said, "Of course Mary."

Mary smiled when she heard him speak her name. She was tired of titles and all the lies that go with them. Here in this place, she would purify herself before God. Picking up the teapot, she began to pour the tea for both of them.

"Jupiter," she said, "did you see when Mr. Montford put his mouth to my ear?"

No longer doubtful about her friendship, but curious about why she did this, Jupiter answered, "Yes Mary, I did see that."

"And did you wonder why I allowed him that liberty?" she asked further.

Jupiter did not want to let her know how much he had doubted her faithfulness and only replied, "I understand fully about having to keep up a pretense."

"Well, it was not merely for the sake of pretense that I allowed it," Mary explained. "At first, he would not tell me what I wanted to know, but I persuaded him by offering him the chance to whisper it into my ear."

Jupiter looked at her in confusion and asked, "What was it that he would not tell you?"

"He would not tell me the name of your father," she said smiling.

Jupiter was in shock. How many times had he passed a field of slaves and wondered if any of those men and women could be his parents, or sisters, or brothers. When he saw a man beaten or whipped in the streets he sometimes wondered, *am I watching my father suffer*. Over the years, he had looked at so many faces searching for something familiar—any hint of something that would say *yes, you are a part of me*. And after all of the years he had spent wondering, to finally learn that the truth was always there, but that it had been intentionally kept from him. If Montford knew, then so did Springsteen. Who else knew the secret that was rightfully his?

Mary worried when she saw the strange look on Jupiter's face, and how he did not speak for what seemed like the longest time. "Are you well Jupiter? Do you wish to know what I have learned?" she asked, now unsure how or even if she should tell him.

Jupiter looked at her, and then passionately grabbed her hand in both of his. "Yes," he said, "you must tell me. I have wondered about this for all of my life."

Mary was not sure how to begin. She did not anticipate how intense this moment would be and was not prepared. Jupiter seemed so vulnerable, and the last thing she wanted was to say the wrong thing. She placed her free hand on top of Jupiter's hands and looked at their four hands that had now become one solid mass. "He was a visitor to the Powel plantation," she said, pausing to gage his reaction.

"What do you mean that he was a visitor?" asked Jupiter who was confused by what she had just said. "Are you saying that my father was not a slave?"

Mary now hesitated to tell him. The last thing she wanted to do was to cause him any pain, but he was waiting for a truthful answer. "Your father was a white man," she quickly said.

There was a look of disbelief in Jupiter's eyes. Mary shifted in her chair. No matter how difficult it would be, she must tell him all that she knew. She owed him that for his gift of friendship.

"When your father was a young man," she explained, "he spent a summer as a guest at the Powel plantation and that is where he..." She paused trying to choose her words carefully. "That is where he became acquainted with your mother." Mary felt foolish describing it this way, but she wanted to deliver the truth as gently as possible.

Jupiter slipped his hands from hers and rose up from the table. He began to pace back and forth on the old wooden floor. It was no surprise to him that many slaves had white fathers, but he never suspected that he was one of them. His dark skin gave no hint of a white man. This news was deeply troubling. If his father had been a slave, at least there would be a connection—father and son who were both forced to live as slaves. But what

111

could it mean for him to have a white man as a father? What possible connection could there be?

"Jupiter," said Mary, rising from her chair and walking towards him, "should I tell you his name? I will tell you that he is alive as we speak. If you would rather not know, I will remain silent. However, I will say it if you wish."

Jupiter thought for a moment. Did he really want to know? What could be gained in knowing the truth? Yet, there were men who knew the truth. Springsteen and Montford had known. How many others knew his secret? He remembered the way the men had mysteriously whispered about him as he stood on the auction block. Now he began to feel angry. How many knew? How many men, who claimed authority over him, knew the name that was rightfully his to know? Jupiter looked at Mary said, "Mary, tell me his name."

Mary felt uncomfortable saying it out loud. Somehow, it just didn't seem right that she should just blurt it out like it had no weight. Surely, it would only fall heavy and hard in the middle of the cabin, and sit there forever unmovable. It had to be passed carefully.

Mary got up and walked over to Jupiter. She stood on her toes to put her lips near his ear. Clearly, so there could be no doubt, she whispered the name. As she pulled back from him, he did not respond in any way, but only remained still and looking down at the floor.

It seemed like a long time before he finally spoke. "I must go," he simply said, and then quickly went out the door.

Mary instinctively knew better than to try and follow him. Instead, she went back to the table and sat down. She looked at the jug of flowers on the table and prayed:

Oh Lord, Defend the poor and fatherless: do justice to the afflicted and needy. Deliver the poor and needy: rid them out of the hand of the wicked. Amen

Chapter 15

When Jupiter suddenly left the cabin, Mary just assumed that he needed time to be alone and had simply returned to his shack. It was not until the morning, when he did not appear with breakfast that she became concerned and went to look for him. When she knocked on the door of the shack there was no answer. She slowly opened it and peered inside. His cot was neatly made up and the kitchen area appeared to be still in disarray from the meal preparation from the night before. She realized then, that Jupiter was gone.

Mary was immediately frightened for his safety. She had enough faith in their friendship that she knew he would not have left her alone in this place, unless he was in serious distress. Where could he be? She prayed that he had not come to any harm.

Knowing how easily she could get lost in a wilderness she did not understand, Mary dismissed any thoughts of trying to search for him. She wanted to be careful not to make the situation any worse. Instead, she completed most of Jupiter's usual morning chores as best she could. After tidying the kitchen, she sat down and waited on an old log near the shack, hoping desperately that he would return soon.

After over an hour of waiting, Mary got tired of sitting on the log and went back to the cabin. She left the door wide open and sat in a chair where she would be able to see outside. Once in a while she would try to keep busy by refolding sheets or clothing, but she found that all she could really do was just wait and worry.

It was past midday when Jupiter finally appeared in the doorway. Mary almost jumped up to embrace him, but thought better of it. It was important that she did not overstep the mark and possibly make it more difficult for him. Instead, she remained calmly seated at the table.

Jupiter entered the cabin and silently sat down with Mary. It was apparent that he had slept little if at all. The whites of his eyes were red with fatigue, and there were several leaves stuck in his hair. His usually immaculate clothes were disheveled and dirty.

"I am sorry Mary," he said, looking directly into her eyes. "I am sorry for running off. I hope that you were not frightened to be left here alone."

The last thing Mary expected was an apology. "No Jupiter, you do not need to apologize to me. You had a shock. Perhaps it is I who should say 'I am sorry.' Perhaps there was a better way to tell you the truth. I should have been more tactful with my words."

"Oh Mary," Jupiter said, shaking his head, "it would not matter what words you chose. Nothing could have prepared me for the truth."

"Where did you go?" asked Mary, as she slowly reached over and gently pulled a leaf from his hair.

Jupiter did not seem to notice her doing this. He only sighed and replied, "I mostly walked along the river. When I had gone so far that I no longer recognized where I was, I turned back. On my way back, I stopped to rest under a tree and that is where I fell asleep. I am unsure just how long I slept, but at first I was awakened several times by discomforting dreams. After the sun had already begun to rise, I fell into an undisturbed sleep and did not wake again until it was high in the sky."

Jupiter leaned his elbow on the table and rested his forehead against his hand. "It was very disconcerting news," he said.

"It was shocking news," said Mary, "and it will take time for you to feel more comfortable with it."

114

"But I should have known," said Jupiter, a little angry at himself for not reading the signs. "There are so many slaves fathered by white men. I should have considered that a possibility. I always knew there was something whispered about me, but I just never thought much about it. And when you told me his name, it was like a dagger to my heart."

Mary was surprised. "You know this man?" she asked.

"I know of this man—and I have seen this man—and this man has seen me," replied Jupiter. "It was only once, but I remember it well. I am sure there are many moments in my life that I have forgotten, but this odd encounter remained in my memory. Only now do I understand why."

"When did you see him?" asked Mary, amazed that Jupiter had once crossed paths with his father.

Jupiter looked at her and sat up straight in his chair. "It was about three years ago that it happened," he said. "Captain Springsteen had been invited to attend a very important meeting. I believe it may have had to do with the war, and it involved the most important men in America. The meeting was to be held at the house of the same man of whom we now speak. Captain Springsteen was extremely excited about the invitation. He is usually excluded from the highest of society. They find him useful for his knowledge and abilities where Indians are concerned, but do not associate with him otherwise.

"As his personal slave, it was my responsibility to drive him out to the grand house. He even rented a fancy carriage for the occasion, not being the sort of man to own one. After we drove up to the house, I remember that the Captain was welcomed in through the front entry, and I took the carriage around to the back where I unhitched the horses and then spent the rest of the time in the yard and kitchen with the other slaves. For me, it was a very uneventful trip except for the strange thing that happened when the meeting was finished, and I took the carriage around to pick up Captain Springsteen.

"I brought the carriage to the front where the men were gathered and bidding each other farewell. Having stopped again in front of the grand entry, I stepped down to open the carriage

115

door for the Captain who was standing nearby with a group of men. That group included the master of the house. I remember how I found it strange the way in which Captain Springsteen called out, "Oh and here is my man Jupiter." The way he said it was very unlike the way he usually spoke. I fully realize that he does take great pride in me as a trophy, and enjoys the envy of gentlemen who see themselves as more deserving than him, but he never really gloated that openly before. With the strangeness of the situation, I forgot myself entirely and looked up at him. This is completely unacceptable for a valet to do. For some unknown reason, I was then drawn to do something that was even more unthinkable. I looked directly at the master of the house. When I looked at that man, I could see that he never hesitated to look right at me. He should have been angry that I should look him in the eye, but he was not. All he did was to stare at me with the stare of a man gazing at a curiosity. He looked at me with such a strange and distant interest that I felt as though he were trying to focus on me through a darkened glass. Our eyes stayed locked for what seemed like a long time, but then the spell was suddenly broken by the sound of Captain Springsteen's voice. At that point, I just turned and opened the carriage door. I did not look up again, and rode off a little shaken and unsure of what exactly had transpired."

The sun was streaming through the cabin window and coming to rest on the center of the table. In the middle of the light was the shadow of the windowpanes. Jupiter absently reached over and placed his hand in the shadow-cross. He looked up at Mary and said, "I never saw that man again, but the exchange was so mysterious and inexplicable that the memory stayed with me. When you said his name yesterday, I at first could not believe it was him. But I then soon realized it was true, and finally understood what had happened that day we looked at each other."

Jupiter curled his hand into a fist, but did not remove it from the shadow. "He knew who I was, Mary. That day he looked right at me and into my eyes—he knew that I was his son—his son living in bondage. He stood there and looked at me as if I were nothing more than an interesting piece of furniture. He watched as I went away with the man who owned me. What kind of a man could do this, Mary? What kind of a man could choose this? I know that many would be proud to have been fathered by such a powerful and important man, but I am not one of those. What pride can I feel in a father who turns his back on his child? What pride can I feel in a man who has gained so much in this world, but has forfeited his own son? Is this what I am born from?" Jupiter folded his arms upon the table and laid his head down upon them.

Mary could see how deeply Jupiter was hurting and desperately wanted to help. "No!" she cried. "Jupiter, you are nothing like your father. You are noble and pure. You were born clean under the laws of God. I look into your eyes and I know who you are. You walk in truth, and with a perfect heart."

Mary again felt the urge to put her arms around Jupiter and try to lessen his pain, but she knew that this would likely upset him even more. Instead, she tried to give him the only comfort in her power to give and said, "I also know who your mother was."

Jupiter raised his head and looked at her. In the distress he suffered from learning about his father, he had forgotten about his mother. Mary did, after all, say that she knew who his parents were.

"I was able to get Mr. Montford to tell me not only her name, but when we walked in the woods I was able to learn as much as he knew about her and her circumstances," said Mary quickly. She could see from his face that Jupiter desperately wanted to know what she had to tell him.

"And...Oh Jupiter," she said, her eyes watering up with tears, "you do remember her."

Jupiter's eyes flashed at her words. How could he remember his mother?

"Your mother was Sarah," she said softly. "The same Sarah you remember playing and singing, and the same Sarah you remember being taken away by Mr. Powel."

Jupiter looked over at the open door of the cabin and could see Sarah's face clearly in his memory. "Sarah? That young girl? The girl, who I remembered all this time, was my mother?" He shook his head and said, "Since I was a boy I wished so much to know what she looked like and all this time, I knew her face—I could not forget her face. She was just so young. I never imagined that she was my mother." Jupiter was overcome with emotion and for the first time Mary saw tears fall from his eyes.

Eager to tell Jupiter everything she had learned, Mary said, "Sarah was born on that plantation to two people who themselves were born in Africa. They were purchased by Mr. Powel's father from a slave ship. Mr. Montford did not know their real names—the names given to them by their own parents, but on the plantation they were called Gideon and Naomi. A few years before you were born, they were given away to a Powel relative in lieu of money owed."

Mary paused, took a deep breath, and then continued with her story. "Sarah remained alone on the Powel plantation. Mr. Montford believes that she was only about eleven years old when her parents were taken away. She was very beautiful and still quite young when she caught the eye of your father. By that time, she was only around thirteen. Mr. Montford could not provide any of the details of the exact nature of the relationship, but could tell me that your father spent a good deal of time in her company. Apparently, the Powel men made great fun out of his attachment to her. After that summer, he never returned to the plantation again.

"Sarah gave birth to you the next spring. Then, when you were almost three years old some trouble began. Mr. Powel started to notice for himself how lovely Sarah was, and when Mrs. Powel learned about his interest she was very upset. She demanded that he sell Sarah as soon as possible. Mr. Powel was apparently quite obedient when it came to his strong-willed wife, and he did as he was told. Sarah was taken to auction within the week. He refused to sell you also, as he would not have gotten a good price for such a small child. Also, because of

118

who your father was, he knew that when you were a little older, your sale would provide him with a higher than usual profit. Apparently, even though the famous parentage of some slaves is said to be secret, men gossip all the time and seem to reveal the truth for sport, for political gain and for profit. I was told that Mr. Powel likely would have kept you longer than he did, as by that time you would be better trained and bring an even higher price, but Mrs. Powel insisted on a quicker sale as you reminded her of Sarah."

Mary stopped speaking. Jupiter did not look at her, but only stared at his arms that lay still crossed on the table. He did not move or say a word.

Feeling that it was best to leave him alone for a while, Mary quietly got up from the chair and went outside. The sun was still shining bright as she walked towards the garden. When she reached it, Mary got down on her knees and began to remove some weeds that had begun to come up around the unfledged vegetables. She felt like crying, but instead comforted herself by praying aloud:

For as the earth bringeth forth her bud, and as the garden causeth the things that are sown in it to spring forth; so the Lord GOD will cause righteousness and praise to spring forth before all the nations.

Chapter 16

The next morning Mary had just finished dressing when Jupiter knocked at the door. She had been afraid that he might suffer a long and intense malaise, but he showed no signs of it when he walked in with the breakfast tray and cheerfully bid her good morning. His hair and clothing were once again immaculate. After setting down the tray on the table, he pulled out the chair for Mary and then sat down himself.

Mary watched as he silently poured the tea. "How are you feeling today?" she asked, curious about how quickly he seemed to have bounced back from what was a terrible ordeal.

Jupiter finished pouring and looked over at her. "I am much better today," he said. "Thank you for asking." He placed a plate of bread and eggs in front of her.

"I was still concerned that I had erred in telling you all that I had found, and that you may not be happy with me today," said Mary, spreading honey on her bread and then offering Jupiter the honey pot.

He accepted the pot and dipped his knife into it. "The truth was always there Mary. And although I did not realize it before, I now know that I was tormented by the constant nagging suggestion of its presence. Prior to you finding what was missing, there was always a sense that there was something just out of reach. You told me what I wanted and needed to know. It just proved to be such a shock for me. If I am to be honest, I did not expect to feel so intensely."

"You must not think that it is a weakness to react the way you did," Mary responded. "It was a perfectly understandable reaction."

Jupiter smiled and said, "You are right Mary. I suppose I was feeling some shame. Men are not expected to lose control of their emotions, and I have always prided myself on maintaining my dignity in the face of overwhelming circumstances. Yet, I should not have expected anything else. For my entire life, I have tried to imagine a mother and a father, and then to find out, not only who they were, but that I remembered them both. It was quite disconcerting. I was also very angry to find out that those around me, like Captain Springsteen, knew my lineage, but kept it from me. It leaves me feeling betrayed. I know it is foolish to feel that way. To them I am only a slave, but still, this is the way I am feeling."

"Why do you think that they would intentionally keep this from you?" asked Mary.

Jupiter took a small bite of the honey soaked bread from his plate, and quickly swallowed it. "I would assume that it is likely a matter of power," he said. "There is always power in knowledge, and that includes the knowledge of one's own history. They are always afraid of losing their power. Brute force can only do so much. Their power must also be sustained by lies. This was just one more lie for them to hold over me."

Mary took a sip of warm tea. Although her world was different from Jupiter's, she understood what he was talking about. She had seen how men ruthlessly seized power and then schemed to hold on to it. "You are very correct about brute force being only one part of the whole," she said. "The entire thing begins with greedy desire and from these seeds spring many forms of oppression. Within a short time, however, the oppressors are themselves transformed. Blinded by their unfulfilled hunger, they do not notice what unnatural things happen to them. The work they do inevitably perfects their imperfections, and then they will even pass this perversity down through the generations. They commit the most horrible sins, and define those sins as good and noble deeds. Even something as obviously vile as enslaving and selling your own children can become defined as a noble venture."

Jupiter nodded his head in agreement. "You are right Mary. Mr. Pierce sells one or two of his children every year. He has a reputation for deliberately siring his own slaves. They say that he first scours the slave markets for girls who have just entered womanhood. He looks for young women because his preference is for virgins. These are the girls he chooses to produce his prize slaves. Whenever he does bring one of his children to auction, he will boast about their breeding. Although he never says outright that he is the father, everyone knows the truth. I have heard that his children usually do go for a higher than average price, so I suppose that Mr. Pierce's ideas on breeding are taken seriously by many."

Mary could eat no more. She knew it was not just about Pierce. He was only one small piece of the larger picture. He just represented how the disease manifests in a single man. The problem was far bigger than that.

Feeling the weight of the dark cloud that now hung in the room, Mary decided she needed to change the subject. There was something that she had wanted to ask Jupiter for a long while, and suddenly thought that this was the perfect time. "Jupiter," she said, "would you please teach me how to fish?"

Jupiter began to laugh and the dark cloud instantly vanished. "You want to fish?" he asked, amused at both her abrupt change of topic and her strange request.

"Well," she said, feigning indignation at his laughter, "this is something I have never done, but have always wondered about. I have read many tales about fishermen, and as a child I wished that I had someone who could teach me. I am quite capable of learning how to fish. Why, yesterday I was able to milk the cow and feed the hens when you were not around. I even considered preparing a chicken for supper."

It was obvious to Jupiter that she was only playfully pretending annoyance at his laughter. He smiled mischievously at her and asked, "You do know that you must first clean the chicken and remove the feathers?"

Mary laughingly replied, "And you believe I am so useless, that I would not even know enough to clean the bird and remove the feathers?"

Jupiter looked at her happy face. It was such a precious gift to be able to joke with someone. In that moment, he felt something he could not remember ever feeling. He felt extremely grateful to another human being. Looking seriously into her eyes he said, "Mary, after all that you have done for me? You have found for me knowledge of immense personal importance—knowledge that I might never have found in my entire lifetime without your help. I thank you from the bottom of my soul, and it would my honour teach you how to fish."

Mary smiled and jumped out of her chair. "Please then, shall we go now? I promise that I shall be a most attentive student."

"Then come with me dear lady." Jupiter stood up and gestured toward the door. "And I shall make you a fisherman."

They both laughed and headed out the door, leaving the breakfast dishes for later.

Over the next few days, Mary and Jupiter had become even closer friends. They worked together as equals and were unafraid to speak openly and honestly with each other. Jupiter had already read through the entire Bible, and they enjoyed many discussions about the various books. Mary continued to teach Jupiter all of the things she had been taught about the world. She made a point of letting him know every story she could remember about Jupiter the god, which sometimes made him laugh so hard that he could barely catch his breath.

One evening as they were just finishing their supper, Mary felt it was a good time to talk with Jupiter about something which had been on her mind for some time. She set her fork down upon her empty plate and said, "Jupiter, you and I have come to be great friends and I want there to be no secrets between us."

Jupiter had just finished off the last of his plate. He could tell from the tone in her voice that she had something very important to say. It worried him a little as to what she could mean by 'secrets.'

"I have told you before about my family as a Royal Family," she said, "but they are more than that. They are considered The Holy Royal Family." Mary paused, uncertain how to say everything that needed to be said. She knew that by revealing her greatest family secret to an outsider, she was also breaking the most sacred rule—a rule she had pledged to live by. But things had changed. Mary needed cast off her shackles, and to do this she must tell Jupiter everything. After all, Jupiter was only an outsider in the world of men. He was not an outsider in the Eyes of God. Taking a deep breath, she said, "You have read through the Bible, but something you would not know is that within some of those pages is a secret story."

Jupiter was surprised by what she had just said. That book was full of some very strange stories that he had read very carefully. He couldn't imagine which ones could hold a secret tale, or how the secret would be hidden there.

"I will show you later how to read the secret story," said Mary, "but for now, I will simply tell you that it is there."

"And what is the story about?" asked Jupiter.

"The story tells of a sacred marriage," replied Mary. "There are many more details that I will share with you eventually, but to get to my point I will talk about what happened after the marriage. What is not recorded in the Bible, but has been handed down through the generations is that this sacred marriage produced a living female child who, as a young girl, fled with her mother to the south of France. When this girl reached womanhood she married and produced children. Today, the many descendants of this woman are known as The Vine. The most important parts of The Vine are those branches that lead unbroken through the female line and back to the first Holy Woman of the sacred marriage. The branches of this family can be found throughout many countries including America. Mine is but one of them, and I am one of those whose ancestry goes directly back from mother to mother to mother and eventually this Holy Woman. That is why I am so important to Mr. Montford, Mr. Pierce and Captain Springsteen. They are members of the Brotherhood. The Brotherhood, among other things, keeps guard over The Vine."

Jupiter occasionally wondered about those men with their strange meetings. Now it was beginning to come clear.

Mary tucked some loose hair up under her bonnet and continued, "As I mentioned before, it is considered important that the members of the family do not marry outside of the bloodlines, but there is more to it. They cannot marry outside of the family because it is believed that by marrying within the family the Holy Marks are preserved."

Jupiter looked at her curiously. "What do you mean by Holy Marks?" he asked.

Mary knew that once she revealed the secret, there would be no return. This was the greatest secret of all time, and it went back well over a thousand years. Countless lives had been sacrificed to keep it safe. She had always been told that it must be kept at all costs, but recently she wondered if hiding this truth caused greater harm than good. Perhaps in the beginning, it was different. Perhaps then, the secret was kept for pure reasons, and allowed the righteous to thrive. But had it all become perverted? Had it somehow turned from a sacred secret kept out of love for God, and into a lie that allows for the reign of murderers and thieves?

She thought of those in her own family who would instantly cut her throat if they knew what she was about to do. Still, here was her dear friend waiting before her—waiting for the truth. She looked into his eyes and said, "There are three Holy Marks. Even though I am considered important to the family, I have none of these and neither does my sister Ann, nor my brother. I cannot say for certain about my parents. Whenever a child is born with one of these marks, that child is considered a Holy Blessing."

"What are these Holy Marks?" Jupiter asked, intrigued by her strange story.

Mary hesitated for a moment. A voice from deep within told her that there was still time to turn back. The secret was still safe. She could just make up anything, and it would be that simple. But then she thought about Jupiter. He spoke openly and honestly in her presence, trusting that she would not betray him. She knew that when he offered her friendship, he risked death. So why should she hesitate risking her life for him? If they were to be true friends then the ground must be leveled and nothing should be hidden. Mary took a deep breath and said, "The first Mark has always been the most likely to occur. It is a tilt to the head. The neck softly curves and the head naturally rests to one side. In some who have it, the head tilts to the right and for others to the left. It is also more noticeable in some than in others."

Mary paused for a moment and then continued on, "The second Mark has to do with the proportions of the subject's body. The body would have very specific and perfect proportions. One aspect is that the entire body would measure an equal distance from the center outward in all four directions. This Mark is referred to as The Divine Proportion or the Golden Mean. There are many old stories about turning lead into gold which secretly refer to the possibility of creating children with such proportions. Any child born with sacred proportions would be considered very important."

Mary waited a moment to see if Jupiter had any questions, but he was silent. "The third Mark," she continued, "is sometimes considered the most sacred of all, and no child has been born with this since—well—anyone can remember. It is known as The Holy Grail. The Holy Grail is like a tiny cup, not much deeper than your palm when you slightly cup your hand." Mary held out her right hand gently cupping it. "Only about as deep as this." she said, tracing the tiny valley with the index finger of her left hand. "There are many stories of The Holy Grail as the cup that caught the blood of Jesus, and it did, but not in the way the stories tell it. The Holy Grail is not a cup

126

that can be held in the hand." Mary briefly paused and just stared at her outstretched palm. "The Holy Grail, my dear friend, is not a cup in the ordinary sense of the word at all. The truth is that The Holy Grail is found in the skull."

"In the skull?" questioned Jupiter.

"Yes," Mary replied, "a tiny cup-like area right at the very center of the skull."

"You mean here?" asked Jupiter touching the top of his head.

"No not there," said Mary, suddenly rising from her chair and at the same time raising her hand to show him exactly where the spot would be. Her movements caught Jupiter by surprise and he instinctively ducked his head as if to avoid being hit.

Mary froze, and then slowly lowered her hand. "Oh Jupiter," she cried, "what have they done to you?!"

"I am sorry Mary," he said, feeling embarrassed. "I know that you would never do anything to hurt me. It was just a reaction. It was nothing to do with you."

"You have no need to be sorry," said Mary, moving around to his side of the table. She stood behind him and explained, "I am going to show you exactly where The Holy Grail is found." Gently she pressed her fingers directly onto the crown of Jupiter's head. "Right here," she said. Her fingers paused there for a moment as she thought how lovely and soft his hair was.

Jupiter felt uncomfortable by this physical contact. He tried not to show it and asked, "What if a child is born with all three of the Holy Marks?"

Mary, who was still standing behind him answered, "Then my dearest friend, the world will be in for quite a change."

Jupiter did not reply, but wondered what she could mean by that. Before he could ask anything more, Mary said, "Jupiter, turn your chair around, as I want to show you exactly what you have come to mean to me."

At first, Jupiter did not move or say a word in response to her request.

"Come now," she gently coaxed, "turn your chair around, please." Jupiter's reaction when she had tried to touch him had deeply upset her. She was determined to make a gesture that would reassure him completely of their friendship. She needed him to know without a doubt that he could trust her.

Jupiter wanted to just leave the room at that moment. Whatever she had planned frightened him and he wanted no part of it. However, he knew that an abrupt departure would certainly hurt her feelings, so he reluctantly he turned his chair to face Mary.

Mary smiled, knowing that it was not easy for him. She was happy that he would go this far for her. Without a word, she went over to the washstand and picked up the basin that was filled with clean warm water. She carried it over and laid it down near Jupiter's feet. She then went over to the cupboard where she took out a white sheet. Kneeling in front of him she gently took off one of his shoes and then the other. Without a word she slowly pulled off his stockings. Then moving the basin over, she placed both of his feet into the water. Carefully and slowly, she began to wash his feet with her hands.

Jupiter did not say a word, but just looked at this woman who humbly knelt before him. Her touch was filled with respect and loving care. What could he say to this? A moment ago he dreaded what she might do, and now he could think of nowhere else he would rather be. A moment ago his veins were filled with the iron that life had put there, and now they warmed with the flow of pure blood. He was surprised when his eyes began to swell with tears.

Mary looked up at him and smiled. She then picked up the sheet she had previously set to one side, and placed it her in her lap. When she lifted his feet from the water, she set them down upon the sheet and wrapped them. She gently dried them, and then tenderly replaced his stockings and his shoes. Still sitting at his feet, she again looked up at him and said, "I am your friend forever, and this moment you will remember always."

Jupiter did not say a word. Somehow, it did not seem right to say anything. Instead, he simply stood, picked up the tray of dishes from the table and returned to his shack.

That night Jupiter lay awake and unable to sleep. He stared at a crack in the wall where a small sliver of moonlight passed into the dark room. Looking at the tiny silvery glow, he found himself thinking about the story of Lazarus who had been entombed in darkness. Jupiter closed his eyes and imagined himself in a sealed cave. His arms and feet are bound with burial cloth and unable to move. His face is veiled with a napkin he cannot see through—alone and dead—dead to everyone. The tomb is silent and cold. There is nothing but dark and empty hopelessness.

But then he hears a small sound—a muffled sound from somewhere outside the stone walls. It is the sound of a woman crying. Is she crying for him? Once there was a woman who had cried like that for him. Sarah, his mother, had cried like that for him the day she was taken away. Tears ran down the sides of Jupiter's face and into his hair. It was then that he was sure he heard a woman's voice say, "Come forth, my son" and the napkin was lifted from his face.

Chapter 17

The following day was wet and dark, but the rain was welcome as it had not rained in over a week, and their small garden was in need of water. After breakfast, Mary said, "Jupiter today is such *a day of clouds and thick darkness.* Once you have finished any necessary chores, please return to the cabin, and we shall keep up our spirits with conversation."

While she waited for Jupiter, Mary tidied the room, pushed the table to the wall and set up two chairs in front of the fireplace. She then lit a small fire to take the damp out. It was the first time that she had ever prepared a fire on her own, and was quite proud when she saw the pretty yellow flames come to life and dance among the logs.

As he approached the cabin, Jupiter was surprised to see the smoke rising from the chimney. He walked through the open door and saw her waiting in the chair. Smiling mischievously he said, "I hope that you did not burn yourself too badly."

"I did not burn myself at all or anything other than the intended wood," she answered, pretending to be indignant over his comment. She pointed proudly at the fire and said, "I ask you sir, have you ever seen a more pleasant fire in your life? Its unique glow is a work of high art, and I do believe that I am now a master of the craft. Up until a few moments ago, I was in total ignorance as to the extent of my talents."

Jupiter laughed and sat down on the chair next to hers. "Well, I suppose it is a fine enough fire."

"Oh it is far more than fine," said Mary laughing. "I believe that you are perhaps jealous of my skill."

"And I believe you may be right," he said with a wink. He then leaned back in his chair and asked, "So, what should we discuss today? I could tell you more about the Indian villages, or would you prefer to tell me some more about the stories from your books?"

Mary hesitated. There was something she very much wanted to talk to him about, but was unsure how to broach the subject. Although they had talked openly about so many things, there was something that remained unsaid. It was the last barrier between them, and she wanted it down. "I think that we should talk again about secrets," replied Mary.

"Secrets? Do you have even more secrets to tell?" he asked with a smile.

Mary folded her hands in her lap and looked at the fire. "I have tried to be honest with you, and have told you every secret I have. I have even divulged the secrets of my family for which I had taken an oath that I would never tell anyone upon the threat of death. But you are not just anyone Jupiter. You are my dearest friend and I am certain that I am yours."

Jupiter was not sure what to say. It was true that she was his friend. He had tried not to think too much about it. To think about it could raise questions in his mind that he did not want to face. Instead, he chose to simply accept this strange friendship as he accepted the air he breathed or the water he drank.

Mary hesitated to say more. She didn't want to drive him away, but she knew that as his friend, she had to say something. Taking a deep breath, she said, "Although there is so much I have learned about you, there is one secret that you still keep from me."

"What secret?" he asked. "I cannot think that I have any secrets to tell." Jupiter was beginning to feel very uncomfortable.

Mary had hoped that he would volunteer to tell her himself, but realized that she would have to force him into being absolutely truthful. She looked him in the eye and said, "In the society that I am from, there are many men who have very limited or no interest at all in women."

Jupiter looked away and into the fire. He now knew what she wanted to talk about. For so many years, he had kept his secret deep within his soul. He struggled to ensure that no small glance in the wrong direction would reveal his true nature to the men who exploited him. As long as no one else knew, he could stay secure within this armor.

Mary could see from the expression on his face and the way he avoided looking at her, that Jupiter just wanted to run straight out of the room. But she was determined to continue.

"The courts of England have plenty of such men, and in my lifetime I have been acquainted with many. Not all of them are the same, and neither are the reasons for their lack of interest. When Captain Springsteen said that you were such a man, I simply accepted this as truth, and you seemed to give no indication to be anyone else. But now, upon knowing you better, I am certain this is not true. This is also the one thing you have not told me about—the one remaining secret that keeps a distance between friends."

Jupiter stared at the now struggling fire. Rising from his chair, he felt the urge to just leave, but instead he added some more wood to keep it burning. He then sat back down, unsure of not only how to begin, but if he should begin at all. More than anything, he wanted to be honest. These past weeks, Mary had helped him see things in a new way. For the first time in his life, he had a taste of real freedom. Yet, there was still so much to fear. Was this feeling of freedom his salvation or his downfall? Was it foolish of a slave to dare to embrace even the smallest sense of freedom? Would this not just lead to agonizing disappointment? Surely, these days would end and he would have to return to his old life.

Mary sighed and said, "Jupiter, I know this has been your deepest secret, but it stands like a wall between us. Please, know that you can trust me. I have already promised to never betray you. Will you please be completely truthful with me?"

Jupiter still stared at the fire. There were now beautiful yellow flames that frolicked and embraced the logs he had placed there. The white smoke danced gracefully upward, disappearing into the darkness of the chimney. He looked over at Mary who was looking at him. Once he said the truth out loud, he would be opening a door that might never be shut again. Yet, he couldn't ignore his strong feelings of wanting more than anything to finally say the entire truth. He had always longed to say it out loud, but had never dared to. Now perhaps, there really was someone in his life whom he could safely tell.

Pushing back the fear that still tried to silence him, Jupiter said, "Mary, you are right. I masquerade as someone who I am not. I am not a man who is without any desire for women. That was a lie I made men believe. I made them believe this so that they would no longer try to trick or force me to produce for them more human chattel. Despite how deeply my heart yearned to touch a woman, I could not unthinkingly take my pleasure and leave behind a son or daughter to suffer life in slavery. It would have killed me to do such a thing. So to protect the innocent, I hid my true nature."

Mary listened and said nothing. The elation that she felt upon hearing Jupiter finally trusting her completely was tempered by the reality of his sad story.

"I could not condemn my own child to a life of suffering, as well as condemn any woman to the suffering of having her child brutally taken from her," said Jupiter, slamming his fist down on the arm of the chair. "As a slave, I am denied all of the freedoms of an ordinary man, and here they had offered up this one highly valued freedom to me. A freedom most men would take in an instant. But if I was to take this freedom, I would be sending my children into slavery. I could not do this Mary." Jupiter sighed and looked at the floor.

Mary could see how painful it had been for Jupiter. Slavery involved the imprisonment of both body and spirit. "It could not have been easy for you," she said, feeling awkward and helpless to bring him any comfort.

"No," Jupiter replied, "it was not easy. There were many times when I was tempted. Thinking I would produce profitable offspring, Captain Springsteen once had me stay alone with a woman for three days. She was very beautiful and I still remember her face well. She was also very innocent and I doubt that she had been with any man before. At first, I tried to explain to her the truth as to why I could not be with her, but she kept insisting that she had a good master who would let me visit her regularly and never sell her children. I could see how much she just wanted desperately to believe that her master was offering her some happiness in her miserable life. It was such a sad thing to see her full of such futile hope, and unable to listen to reason.

"Finally, I gave up trying to be truthful with her and made up a story that all my life I have never had any interest in women, and was certain that I never would. I suppose I must have been convincing as she believed me, and told both her master and Captain Springsteen.

"After that, I was surprised by how much easier my life became. White people seemed more cordial and relaxed in my presence. I was able to enjoy many small benefits because of this new trust in me. There were also more and more requests to hire me out to serve at special occasions, and Captain Springsteen received several offers of purchase. I was suddenly not simply a very good valet, but had now become their perfect Negro."

Jupiter paused and shook his head. Saying those words aloud suddenly made him realize how much he now deplored the idea of the perfect slave, even though he had lived it every day. "It was not always easy to keep this secret," he continued. "But whenever I felt tempted, I would simply touch the scar on my leg from where Mr. Lynch had wounded me, and this would remind me of the real world. This was a physical reminder of all of the horrible things I have suffered and have seen others suffer. This made me think about the children that could face the same fate or even worse, and it was this that helped quell any desire I may have felt."

Mary closed her eyes and tears fell down her face. Sometimes the weight of a heartless world seemed overwhelming. Why was it like this? How do you find God in a world where only oppression seemed to thrive? She opened her eyes and saw Jupiter looking at her. He was waiting for her to say something.

"Thank you," she said sincerely. "Thank you for giving me the gift of your complete trust. I realize that it was not easy for you to do, but your courage has given us both a new freedom. *Truth will set us free*, and today, within this humble little cabin you have provided for us a safe home in a world that otherwise offers no safety. Thank you my friend. You are my *light in the darkness.*"

Chapter 18

Two days passed and Mary and Jupiter continued to enjoy the increased sense of freedom their growing friendship had given them. There was no worry about saying or doing the wrong thing. They were completely open within each other's company.

That morning, as they worked together in the garden, Mary told Jupiter that she wished to go on a picnic. "I did love going on picnics back in England, and it is such a lovely day that I insist we go this afternoon," she said with determination.

Jupiter smiled and shook his head, "I cannot see much point in eating food sitting uncomfortably on the ground when we have a perfectly good table and padded chairs."

Mary was not going to let him talk her out of what she felt was a wonderful idea. "Have you ever been on a picnic before?" she asked.

"I have served at a number of picnics," he replied.

"Serving at one and going on one is not the same thing. Today, I shall take you on your very first picnic, and you shall not be required to serve a thing. You shall merely enjoy yourself and understand why a picnic is fun," said Mary cheerfully.

Jupiter was still skeptical, but he could see that she was not going to let it drop. He began to think that he might as well just go along with the idea. After all, if it didn't require any preparation by him anyway, there was no point in making an issue of it. "And you will prepare everything, and serve the food, and nothing shall be required of me?" he asked.

"You my dear friend need only rest," she replied. "This is to be your first picnic so I will gladly make all of the preparations. Sir, I am inviting you on a picnic, so do tell me, what is your answer?"

Jupiter knew from the tone of her voice that his only option was to surrender. "Then I shall certainly not refuse such a gracious invitation. Yes, I will attend," he said with a bow.

Mary already knew that the best picnic spot could be found down near the river. When she walked there with Mr. Montford, she had noticed a perfect place, where soft green grass grew beside an old oak tree. The wild and natural beauty of this location definitely rivaled any of the well-tended picnic spots she had known back in England.

When sun had reached its highest point, they headed down to the river. Jupiter carried the food which was bundled together in a cloth, and Mary carried a pitcher of milk and a folded white sheet draped over her arm. Although Mary had enjoyed lavish picnics back in England, where she was served a wide array of exotic food, she felt that they could not begin to compare to the simple meal she had packed of bread, honey-butter, and wild strawberries.

"This is the place," said Mary, when they arrived at the old oak tree.

Jupiter knew this spot well. It was here that he had found refuge after learning the name of his father. The gentle sight and sound of the river had soothed and helped him, to finally lie down and sleep. He smiled at the thought that she had chosen this special place.

"Could you take this sheet please and spread it on the ground," Mary requested.

He set down the bundle of food, and took the sheet from her arms. They watched the white linen fly up into the air, and then gently float downward to settle delicately on the soft grass. Jupiter took the milk jug from Mary so that she could sit without the risk of spilling it. Once seated, she then took the jug back from him so that he might also easily sit.

After finding a level spot on the ground to set the milk, Mary then reached for the bundle of food and began to unwrap it. She set out everything as decoratively as possible and then said to Jupiter, "Please, you first."

Mary waited while Jupiter took a piece of bread and spread it with honey-butter. Only after he took his first bite, did she take some for herself. They sat silently eating and looking at the river. Mary went to reach for the milk jug and suddenly realized that she had brought nothing to pour it into.

"Oh my," she said, "I tried to make everything as perfect as possible, but I have forgotten to bring cups for the milk." She felt a little embarrassed that she had not remembered something so basic on the first picnic she had ever organized. Determined that the afternoon would not be ruined by a small mistake, Mary shrugged and said, "Well, we shall just have to share." She then took a drink from the jug and handed it to Jupiter.

Jupiter took it in his hands, but hesitated to put it to his lips. To take a drink from the same jug as Mary was unthinkable in his world. Even though he now saw her as his friend and equal, for a brief moment those voices invaded his mind. They were voices of shame that told him he had no right to anything—including a simple drink from this jug. Jupiter was surprised that these demons had unexpectedly surfaced. He thought that he had control, but in this moment realized that it would require strength and work to take back his life completely. Rebuking those voices, Jupiter put the jug to his mouth, and with pride and determination, quenched his thirst.

It made Mary happy to see Jupiter drink without reserve. "You see," she said, "a picnic is a very enjoyable thing. I know that you were unsure it would be worth the effort, however, you must admit it is quite lovely and peaceful here."

"Yes," Jupiter agreed, "I do like this place." He then set down the almost empty milk jug and casually took off his coat placing it neatly beside him.

Mary handed him a plate with three slices of bread covered in honey-butter and strawberries. She watched as Jupiter swiftly ate them all. For Mary, it was wonderful to see him savor his food so freely. She remembered how, in the beginning, he could barely eat in front of her.

Jupiter looked at his empty plate and his first thought was to find more. Then he looked over at Mary and realized that she had yet to take even a single bite of hers. He began to laugh out loud. "I am so sorry Mary," he said, still laughing. "I have been so rude."

Mary was now laughing also. "Be as rude as you like Sir," she said. "After all, we are eating on the ground. How formal must we be?"

Jupiter grabbed another slice of bread and dramatically tore it with his teeth. They both continued to laugh for what seemed like a long time.

After their laughter had died down, Jupiter stretched out his legs then placing his hands behind his head, he laid back onto the soft white sheet. "Yes," he said, "this was a very good idea." He looked up at the leaves that gently swayed above him. He could hear their gentle rustling whispers and within a short time he had fallen asleep.

Jupiter was sitting on a wooden chair in the Powel's kitchen. He looked around the room and felt good that everything appeared to be in its rightful place. Martha was facing towards him, but was looking down at some bread dough she was kneading on the table in front of her. Jupiter felt hungry as he waited impatiently for her to finish making the bread.

Martha was talking to him about the Powel family. "Dey's eatin' dirt agin," she said.

Jupiter looked out of the window and saw Mr. and Mrs. Powel and their young children in the yard. They were all on their hands and knees, and were licking up dirt like cats licking up spilled milk. Their faces were filthy, and their eyes were frighteningly wild and empty. Jupiter felt disgusted and looked away.

139

Suddenly, he was no longer in the kitchen, but was now in Mr. Lynch's barn. Simon was there, but huddled in a corner and crying. Jupiter saw that the barn door was open and knew that this was his chance to finally get away. He called to Simon, but Simon refused to move. Knowing that Mr. Lynch would soon be returning and the chance for escape would soon be gone, Jupiter walked out and into the sunlight.

When he stepped outside, he found himself standing beside the river. He saw the picnic sheet on the ground near the oak tree, but Mary was nowhere to be seen. He looked in the distance and saw her faraway in a field picking flowers. She waved to him and he waved back.

He then turned and looked at the river. There he saw a small boat coming towards the shore. As the boat got closer, he saw it was his mother, Sarah. Her face was the same as the day she had been taken away, but today she was happily smiling. As the boat came into the shore, he could see that she had a loaf of bread in her hands. Sarah held it out to him. "Here," she said, "you left before Martha had finished. This is yours."

Jupiter took the bread and looked into his mother's happy eyes. He then turned to the oak tree and sat down leaning his back against the trunk. Taking a bite from the loaf, he could not believe how wonderful it tasted. Jupiter looked up and saw Sarah waving to him from the boat as it floated on down the river. He waved back and a feeling of warmth and harmony filled his spirit.

Jupiter opened his eyes and saw Mary's smiling face above him. She softly asked, "Did you sleep well?"

He saw that she had a tiny flower in her hand which she reached over and placed in his hair.

Still groggy from sleep he asked, "What are you doing?"

"I am adorning you," she answered. "Jupiter, you have the most beautiful hair. God certainly created it this way to be adorned, and that is what I am doing. I am doing God's work."

Jupiter sat up and put his hand to hair. He could feel that it was full of little flowers. Imagining what a sight he must be, he began to laugh. "Are you trying to make me into a woman?" he asked.

"No," she said without laughing, "I am adorning you as my bridegroom."

Jupiter could see the serious look on her face. He tried to make light of the situation and nervously smiling said, "You mean to marry me? Well, if you wait here I shall go and get Reverend Ward to marry us, and perhaps Mr. Pierce would be our honoured guest."

Mary did not laugh. Instead, she took his hand in hers and said, "And what are those men in the Sight of God? How could any marriage performed by Reverend Ward be a real marriage when the man is completely unholy?"

Jupiter looked at his hand in hers. He wanted to pull it away and leave, but he did not.

"When I look at you Jupiter," continued Mary, "I see a man who is more worthy than any I have ever seen before. You love truth and goodness, and you fill me with hope. Jupiter, you make me feel that God is always with me—with us. I want to marry only you, and I know with all of my heart that it is God's Will."

Jupiter said nothing. He tried not to look at her, and kept his eyes fixed on the river.

Mary would not be put off by his silence. "Our chapel," she said, "is all of this glorious creation that surrounds and cradles us. Our priest is this beautiful old tree who knows more about love and sanctity than any wicked priest of man. Our guests are the birds and flowers. Our music is the sweet gentle song of the river. Oh Jupiter, marry me!"

Jupiter still did not look at her. He had crossed so many boundaries already, but this one was terrifying. This was a point at which there was absolutely no return. How could any of this be anything more than a mere fantasy? He knew how the real world was, and had never fooled himself about it before. What kind of a dream world was he being pulled into? He put his hand on his thigh and touched his scar to remind himself about what was real.

This did not go unnoticed by Mary. She quickly reached over, took his hand away and placed hers there instead. Through his breeches, she could feel the large crescent shaped ridge left behind by the wound. "No Jupiter," she cried, looking into his eyes and forcing him to look into hers, "no more. We must refuse to accept the lies and evil of mankind. You and I have both been prisoners for all of our lives, but no more. God has offered to set us free and we must not reject this. You are my bridegroom, and although at first I was blind, I see that this is the truth. You, Jupiter, are mine as I am yours. God calls us and it is our duty to follow."

Jupiter heard the sounds of the river grow louder. It seemed to be speaking to him in a language he almost understood. The world began to spin out of focus, and he trembled like a leaf in the wind. He closed his eyes and tried only to concentrate on his own breathing. All he wanted was darkness, but the light shone through and forced his eyes open again. Suddenly, all those things that weighed down his heart and kept him in his designated place—all those things that threatened to crush and suffocate his spirit—all those things that made him forget the man he was, swirled upwards and in an instant disappeared into emptiness.

Now, he could see only her face before him. This was the face of a woman who saw him clearly, for the man that he was. This was a woman who was willing to sacrifice everything to be with him. She was bestowing on him the greatest honour she could offer.

With a light and open heart, Jupiter was suddenly filled with the courage of love. Softly he put his lips to her ear and whispered, "Yes Mary, I cannot deny it any longer. I am your husband."

Gently placing his hand on the nape of her neck, he drew her mouth towards his. A bird flew overhead and its shadow washed over them. Under the warmth of the summer sun, Jupiter offered himself, body and soul, upon God's most sacred altar.

Chapter 19

It was a grey place, and Mary found herself facing a pathway with tall stone walls on either side. As she took a step forward, flowers of beautiful and unimaginable colors sprung from the ground to her right and to her left. Each lovely blossom released a puff of silver dust that floated upward, and then rained down all around her. She continued to walk along the path, and more and more flowers shot up with every step she took. Every blossom continued to release its glowing spores, and soon her hair and gown were completely covered in the bright silver powder.

Mary kept walking until she came to the very end. There, in front of her, was a giant golden rose. She had never seen anything more beautiful in her life. Suddenly, from within the center of the rose, a silver star shot out and high into the air. It disappeared into the sky. Then another and another star leapt forth until there were so many that Mary was blinded by their brilliance. She did not know how much more of this magnificent wonderment she could bear when her eyes suddenly opened, and she saw the morning light shining in through the cabin window.

For a short time, she did not move and just stared at the sunlight. Then slowly, she sat up in the bed, and placed her bare feet on the wooden floor. She looked down at her naked body, and then looked up to see her shift slung over the back of the nearby chair. Mary made a move to reach for it, when suddenly a serpent encircled her waist and held her tightly in place. She smiled and said, "I was just going to prepare us a meal."

Jupiter sat up behind her keeping his arm tightly around her. He kissed her shoulder and said, "Stay a little longer here. Then we shall both go and prepare our meal together."

Mary sighed and leaned back against him. Could anyone be happier than she was at that moment? She spoke aloud the words than came to her mind,

As the apple tree among the trees of the wood, so is my beloved among the sons. I sat down under his shadow with great delight, and his fruit was sweet to my taste.

She slowly turned her face and put her lips to his.

The next few days Jupiter and Mary could not bear to be out of each other's sight, and only managed to do the most essential chores. Their love had opened up a world that neither had ever imagined possible. The sun was brighter, all of the colors more vivid, and every creation of God, no matter how insignificant, somehow revealed its glory and worth. Together, they were a living light that shone on everything that surrounded them.

Late one day, Mary was preparing a small fire as it had turned cold and rainy. She was wearing only her shift as she knelt before the fireplace. Jupiter lay in the bed propped up by the pillows and with his hands behind his head. They had spent most of the afternoon there.

"Will you not get up and help me with the fire?" Mary asked playfully.

Jupiter smiled and replied, "It is the bed, my wife. I cannot bring myself to leave such luxury as this."

"So you will not get up and help me?" Mary coyly asked again. "I think perhaps it is the bed you love and not me." She

145

softly laughed as she placed more kindling upon the little flame she had created.

"Well it is much finer than the miserable little cot they gave me," Jupiter replied laughingly. "Had I known how soft it was, I might have married you sooner."

The fire was now burning nicely. Mary stood up and walked over to the bed. She lay down beside him and placed her head on his chest. The strong rhythmic beat of his heart was a precious comfort, yet at the same time seemed to drum a warning. Mary thought about how they must finish their escape plan as soon as possible.

"Jupiter, in two days Mr. Montford will return," she said. "We do not have much time left to complete the preparations for our journey."

Jupiter took his hands from behind his head and caressed her back. "We will have to take great care to prepare ourselves for his visit. There must be nothing that could make him suspicious. As soon as he goes, we will pack what we need, and then leave the following evening."

Mary smiled at the thought of being free with Jupiter. "Yes," she added, "it will be weeks before his next visit, and we will be far away by the time he returns."

Jupiter stroked her hair and said, "I have been thinking more about the direction we should take. South is far too dangerous. Our only choices are west or north. If we go west, we may find a safe place in the wilderness, but there are also an increasing number of frontiersmen pushing that way. Furthermore, when they come looking for us, they will certainly look to the west before any other direction.

"North is difficult, in that there are more people and towns along the way, but once we get through the most populated areas, I believe that we could find a safe place. As I have never been farther north than Maryland, I cannot say for sure what we will find there. It is a difficult choice my wife. No matter which we chose it will be a dangerous journey."

Mary kept her ear to Jupiter's heart and said, "There was a story told to me many times as a child. It was about two little

146

sisters. One of the sisters always dressed in white and the other always dressed in red. Their names, fittingly enough, were Rose White and Rose Red. The two girls lived happily with their parents until one day when their mother became sick and died. After she died, their father married a widow who had a son. The widow wanted to do away with the girls so that only her son would eventually inherit their father's fortune. She hired a wood cutter to take them to the forest and kill them. The wood cutter took them to the forest, but did not have the heart to kill them. Instead, he abandoned them there with only a single loaf of bread to share between them. Left completely alone, the girls were frightened and did not know which way to go. As they tried to decide their path, a little bear came along. At first they were frightened, but soon realized that he was playful and friendly. They played with him a while, and then shared with him their only loaf of bread. The little bear was grateful for their kindness and before he left, he pointed the direction in which they should go. The girls did follow the bear's instructions and eventually came upon a beautiful castle. It turns out that the castle belonged to their aunt who did not know of her sister's death. She recognized her nieces and welcomed them. And there they lived happily ever after."

Jupiter laughed, "Well that is a fine story, but are you trying to tell me that all we need is to find a little bear to tell us the way to go?"

Mary loved to feel his chest rise and fall as he laughed. It made everything seem like it would be alright. She sighed and said, "We already know Little Bear, my love. He is in the sky and his tail points the way to go."

Chapter 20

When the day of Montford's visit arrived, Mary and Jupiter worked tirelessly to ensure that there were no visible signs of their marriage. They talked about and even practiced their expected roles. If they were to escape, Mr. Montford should not be given even the smallest hint of their true situation. Even though Mary had now enjoyed the freedom of never wearing stays, she decided to wear them in order to reinforce a sense and a look of traditional order. They would also be an uncomfortable reminder that she must maintain the masquerade at all costs.

It was a dull day, and the drizzling rain was unceasing. Jupiter knew that the tea would have to be served inside the cabin, so he made certain that everything was perfectly neat and tidy, and that there were absolutely no signs of him staying there.

As they waited for Mr. Montford to arrive, Mary sat in the cabin with the door open, and Jupiter remained in the old shack. At the sound of the wagon, Mary came out onto the porch and was relieved to see that once again Mr. Pierce had managed to muscle his way in. After the last visit, she had been a little worried that Mr. Montford would want to take his advances to a new level, and it would be too great an effort to have to feign interest in a courtship while, at the same time, keeping him at a distance.

Mary smiled and remained under the shelter of the porch. "Good day gentlemen," she said graciously.

Both men wore large black hats and capes to keep them dry. It was Pierce who was driving the horses and before he could even bring the wagon to a complete stop, Montford had jumped down and leapt onto the porch.

"My Lady," he said, sweeping his hat off of his head with one hand and grabbing her hand to kiss with the other. His lips and face were cold and damp.

Pierce was annoyed. From the way Montford acted, he knew that he must have made some progress with the woman during the previous visit. Pierce had already suspected that the shipment problems that had kept him too busy to see her last time may have been Montford's doing. Now he was certain.

Jupiter appeared near the wagon, and dutifully waited for instructions from Pierce. Mary saw him standing alone in the rain and wished that he at least had a cloak. She then looked quickly away not wanting to raise suspicions.

Handing the reigns to Jupiter and stepping down from the wagon, Pierce looked at Mary and bowed slightly. "My Lady, it is a pleasure to see you again," he said. He then turned to Jupiter and barked, "Take care of the horses and unload the supplies."

Pierce came onto the porch, and Mary watched as Jupiter led the horses around the cabin and towards the barn. "Please do come in," she asked Pierce and Montford as she gestured and stepped across the threshold.

While still on the porch, both removed their capes and hats, and hung them on hooks so as not to drip water all over the cabin floor. When they entered, Pierce rushed to pull out a chair for Mary, and then quickly sat down himself. For a moment, Montford found himself left awkwardly standing. As he took his seat, he felt deep regret that his plan to leave Pierce behind had not worked this time.

There was a large fire burning in the fireplace, and the men relished the warm dry air after their cold rainy journey. Both noticed how tidy and orderly the cabin was. It seemed that the woman was thriving. At various times, they also both allowed their eyes to linger on her bed.

149

Mary hated that they were there—in the cabin that she and Jupiter shared. She wanted to chase them out like vermin, but instead she put on a smile and asked, "I trust that you are both well?"

Before Pierce could open his mouth, Montford replied, "In your presence Lady Mary, how could any man not be well."

Pierce was taken aback that Montford should be so forward in his company. He wanted more than anything to put him in his place, but he knew he had to show restraint and patience—at least for now. Instead, he tried to focus only on Mary and said, "Thank you for asking Lady Mary. Things have been very good for me. I would, however, like to apologize for my absence last time. I very much wanted to enjoy your company again, but when you have a business as substantial as mine, there are many demands."

"Well, I am certainly pleased that you are both here now," she said, wondering how she was ever going to get through this afternoon.

Jupiter suddenly appeared in the doorway with the tea tray covered by a cloth to keep it dry. Mary wanted only to run to him and throw her arms around him. Instead, she kept her eyes on Pierce and Montford, afraid that even a small glance Jupiter's way would cause her masquerade to fall apart.

Without a word, he placed the tray on the table and removed the cloth. He began to set out the cups, but Mary thought it best that he not remain in the cabin any longer than was necessary. "You may go now," she said quickly, trying as best she could to keep her voice cold and commanding. She then turned to Montford and with a smile said, "Mr. Montford would you please serve the tea."

Montford was delighted as he took this a sign of her favor. "It would be my pleasure," he said, as he happily picked up the teapot and began to pour tea into her cup.

The afternoon dragged on as Mary pretended to enjoy the mundane conversation and subtle advances of both men. She was glad that there was no reason for Jupiter to return to the cabin, but at the same time she missed him terribly.

When she felt it was getting close enough to the time when the men should be leaving, Mary said, "This has been such a lovely afternoon gentlemen. It is a great hardship for me to be without company and to have two visitors in one day has been a great pleasure indeed. However, I am afraid that this dreary weather is wearing on me and I am feeling rather fatigued."

"My dear Lady Mary, I assure you that the pleasure has been all ours," said Montford. He was disappointed that the afternoon was coming to an end so soon. Still, there was very little he could say to the woman with Pierce around. Next time, he would definitely make certain that Pierce was busy. It was imperative that, on the next visit, he have the opportunity to openly declare his love. With the war now officially ended, and many rumors circulating, it was unclear what would happen next. He had to move quickly. To add to the urgency of it, the Duke had sent him a letter stating that he wanted her returned to England, but some in the highest ranks of the American Brotherhood had recently taken an interest in her remaining in the new Republic. Montford knew that he might not have much time to win her hand in marriage. He had to play his cards right.

A little too forcefully, Montford slapped his hands on the arms of his chair and exclaimed, "Well, Mr. Pierce, although it is always sad to bid farewell, perhaps it is time that we take our leave."

Pierce did not object, as he was quite ready to go. He was feeling very confident that everything was going according to his plan. Within the last few weeks, he had become privy to secrets that Montford did not know about—secrets that would change a lot of things within the Brotherhood. "If you will excuse me, My Lady, I will have the slave prepare the horses," said Pierce, grinning at Mary. He was now so sure of himself that it did not bother him to leave Mary and Montford alone. In fact, it was pleasing to him that his brief absence would likely leave Montford with a false sense of security.

As Samuel Montford watched Pierce go out the door, he was thrilled that he would have a few moments alone with

151

Mary. Under the table he carefully slid his foot over to gently touch hers.

Mary felt his foot and wanted only to move hers away, but she didn't. She realized that the tiniest gesture could jeopardize their escape. Instead, she reminded herself to be patient and calm. In just a few more minutes, Montford and Pierce would be gone, and she would never have to see either of them again.

"Lady Mary," said Montford, grinning and leaning across the table towards her, "It has been such a pleasure to see you again. My only regret is that we were unable to be alone. Unfortunately, Mr. Pierce feels a duty to be here also. I have told him that it is not fair on Mrs. Pierce that he is away from home so often, whereas I sadly have no one waiting for me to return."

Mary smiled back at him and playing along said, "Dear sir, if next time you come alone then we shall be able to talk more freely." She saw the excited ambition in Montford's eyes, and imagined what a shock it would be when he rode up to the cabin only to find that she and Jupiter were gone.

Montford said a little too enthusiastically, "Yes, My Lady, next time it shall be just you and I." He took her hand in his and kissed it.

Mary looked at him and smiled, hoping that he would not recognize her false affection. This, however, was not a problem as Montford was far too blinded by his own intense desires to see anything but what he wanted to see. He was convinced that he was only steps away from a wedding proposal, and was almost giddy at the thought.

Suddenly, they heard shouting from outside. Mary got up quickly and ran over to the open door of the cabin. Montford followed behind. From the porch, Mary could see only Pierce, in his dark cloak and hat, standing in the drizzle. He was angrily yelling, "I will teach you your place, and you will never forget it!"

Mary stepped out into the rain, and was horrified by what she saw. Jupiter was face first against a tree trunk with his hands tied to a branch above his head. His shirt had been torn up the middle, exposing his back. Mary then looked again at Pierce, and that is when she saw the whip in his hand. In panic, she screamed and ran towards Jupiter. Before she reached him, his eyes flashed a warning and reminded her to keep her head.

Instead of running straight to Jupiter, Mary stood between him and the whip. She looked at Pierce and fell upon her knees in the mud. Clasping her hands together as if in prayer she cried, "Oh Mr. Pierce, you cannot do this to me! I need this slave if I am to survive alone here in the wilderness! You must not punish me like this, I beseech you!"

Pierce silently laughed. He enjoyed seeing her on her knees before him. "Lady Mary, you do not understand about these things," he said. "Slaves require discipline, and this boy has been out here enjoying the easy life too long. He is getting disrespectful, and I fear that he may turn disrespectful to you. I am doing this only for your sake."

Mary could see how much he was enjoying this, but she was prepared do whatever it took to protect Jupiter. Looking briefly at Mr. Montford, she was hoping that he would at least intervene on her behalf, but instead he just stood there like a coward. "Please Mr. Pierce," she said, "what if you do more harm than you intend and he becomes sick. What am I to do alone out here with only a sick or dying slave? Have I not suffered enough? Please, this frightens me."

Pierce was feeling even more excited by her pleading. "Lady Mary," he replied, "I have done this hundreds—perhaps thousands of times. I know what I am doing. The slave will be fine. In the end, he will just be better behaved."

Mary could see this was getting her nowhere. She could not let him harm Jupiter, and Montford had still said nothing. Should she try pleading to him more or would that just drive his bloodlust even further? She decided that there was only one possible way to stop him. Getting up from the ground she moved towards Pierce and threw her arms around his neck resting her head upon his shoulder. "Please Mr. Pierce," she begged, "I beseech you, for my sake, please do not do this! The slave has never shown me any signs of disobedience. He is trustworthy. Out here I am a woman alone, and my fears of not surviving in this wilderness have grown. I am terrified if he should die. If just to ease a poor woman's irrational fear, please do not do this. I beg of you!"

Pierce put an arm around her waist and she felt him press his breeches against her skirt. He looked smugly over at Montford, whose face visibly revealed his jealous anger. Pierce was thrilled by what had happened. Mary removed her arms from around his neck, but he did not let go of her right away. Instead he hung on to her in the pretense of comforting her. "Very well My Lady," he said, "I can see how frightened you are, and this does concern me. To calm your fears, today I will not whip the slave."

Mary sighed in relief. She wanted to push him away in disgust, but instead she stayed her ground and said, "Oh Mr. Pierce, you are so very gracious and kind. I cannot tell you how much relief you bring to my heart. I am forever in your debt."

Pierce triumphantly looked over at Montford who looked away. He was slow to release Mary from his grip, but eventually he could no longer avoid it. When he did, she quickly stepped back from him. Her gown was completely rain-soaked and she shivered with the cold that now seeped into her skin.

Montford, unsure how to redeem himself, tried to heal his wounded pride by walking over to the tree and cutting Jupiter loose. Perhaps this might have some heroic value in Mary's eyes. "Go to your shack, and remain there until Lady Mary tells you otherwise," he commanded Jupiter, who kept his eyes to the ground and without a sound hurried away.

Pierce still enjoying the feeling of being in complete control, said to Mary, "You must go inside now and get warm and dry." He offered her his arm, which she reluctantly took. He then walked her towards the cabin.

Montford followed behind in frustration. He had always been aware of Pierce's high ambitions within the Brotherhood, and in the past was able to keep them in check. Now, he was beginning to see that those ambitions were stronger than he ever imagined. This was not good news, and he wondered just how far he would be forced to go, to keep Pierce from gaining power.

Once Mary was inside the cabin and drying out in front of the fire, Montford and Pierce again bid their goodbyes. She just barely stomached their farewell kisses to her hand and put on a face suggesting that she would miss their company. As soon as she heard the wagon pull out, she jumped from her chair and ran to the shack. She flung open the door and saw Jupiter sitting on the old cot where he used to sleep. He had changed into dry clothing. She threw herself upon him and cried, "Oh my dear husband, did he hurt you? Are you hurt anywhere?" Her eyes combed every inch of him, but it was difficult to see in the dark shed whether or not Jupiter had suffered any wounds.

"I assure you that I am fine," he replied, much to her relief. "My wrists are a little sore and bloody, but that is all."

"Jupiter, I am so sorry that I embraced that man. Please forgive me," she said, now sitting beside him on the cot and leaning against him.

Jupiter wrapped his arm around her. Her dress was still wet and cold. "You did what you had to. You showed courage, and I am proud of you Mary."

Mary sighed, "Our escape will not be easy but I am prepared to do anything to be with you. My love, I know now more than ever that I cannot live without you."

Jupiter hugged her closer. "Your clothes are wet," he said, "and you are shivering. Let us go back to our little house where, for now, we are safe. Tomorrow we will pack our things, and by the evening we will have departed this place forever."

Mary turned her face up towards him and kissed him on his mouth. She then whispered, "Oh my love, if we had the *wings of a dove* we could fly away and find peace."

"Dear Mary, you must know that we already soar through the sky," Jupiter said, caressing her cheek with the back of his hand. "No matter what may happen, we have given each other wings of gold, and no one has the power to ever take that from us."

Chapter 21

Mary was busy picking out the few pieces of clothing that she would take with her. She set aside anything that could not possibly be essential to her new life. She wasn't sure what that new life would entail but she did know that stays would certainly not be a part of it. All she really cared about was that she and Jupiter would be together. Everything else was unimportant.

Her life in England was gone forever and she was glad of this. Except for Ann, what was left there? Only cold halls full of empty echoes that could not possibly compare to the beautiful enduring light of the love she had found in this wilderness. She thought of all of those people that she had known back in the courts. If they ever learned of what she had done, they would assume that she had gone completely mad. She could hear them now—gorging themselves on their gossip. *"They spend their days in wealth, and in a moment go down to the grave,"* she said under her breath, and continued to sort out her belongings.

Jupiter was away in the woods checking some snares. They were to leave that night and they needed to carry as much food with them as was possible. The fresh meat would be good for a day or two, and they had already stocked up on plenty of dried fish and berries, as well as some smoked venison.

Mary had just finished tying up her bundle of clothes in a sheet, when she heard the sound of a horse coming into the yard. She nervously placed the bundle in a corner and threw a cloth over it. Quickly, she went over to the door and opened it just enough to peek out.

Mary didn't know whether to be relieved or alarmed by what she saw. It was James Pierce tying the reigns of a large black steed to a nearby tree. Realizing that she had no alternative but to find out what he wanted, she opened the door wider, but stood blocking the threshold.

Pierce finished securing the horse and then looked over and grinned at the sight of Mary. "My Lady," Pierce said, confidently taking off his hat and bowing. He was definitely trying his best to be charming.

"Mr. Pierce, why are you here? I was not expecting you for another three weeks," said Mary, hoping that she did not sound too anxious.

"I had to come to tell you of something that I could not say in front of Mr. Montford," he said, leaping up on the porch and standing too close for Mary's comfort, "There has been some news from England, and although your brother the Duke gave strict instructions that you were not to know it, in good conscience I could not keep this information from you."

Mary was beginning to feel even more distressed. She sensed something was terribly wrong and wanted to sit down. However, because Pierce would surely follow her into the cabin, she was determined to remain strong and stand in the doorway.

"What is it?" she asked, hoping that he would just tell her quickly and go.

Pierce suddenly grabbed her hand and said, "My Lady, it is your sister Ann. Mr. Montford had received word several days ago that your sister is dead. It is said that she took her own life." Pierce waited for a reaction. He thought that if Montford's coward-like behavior yesterday didn't put a wedge between him and the woman, knowing that he had kept this news from her certainly would.

"Oh God, no!" said Mary, having difficulty believing what she had just heard. "This cannot be true Mr. Pierce. Please tell me that you are confused. My dear sweet Ann cannot be gone." Her legs felt numb and she wasn't sure if she would be able to stand much longer.

Pierce was enjoying every minute of this. Still hanging on tightly to her hand, he said, "Mr. Montford has chosen to obey your brother who does not want you to know. I, however, could not in good conscious keep this from you. I have come here today risking the ire of your brother because it is against my nature to have such a noble lady treated so poorly. Your sister is dead and you have a right to know this."

Pierce waited in anticipation for his words to take full effect. He was delighted when Mary began to weep openly. "Oh Lady Mary," he said, putting both of his arms around her in feigned sympathy.

Mary pulled back immediately, but found he would not release her. "Please Mr. Pierce," she said, "I feel as though I cannot breathe. Please, I must have some space."

Reluctantly, he released his grip. Mary stepped backwards, and found herself just inside the door of the cabin. Learning of her sister's death was devastating, but she had to focus on her own survival now. She needed to keep a clear head, and Pierce had to be gotten rid of as quickly as possible.

"I am so grateful for your honesty sir, but I think that I must now be left alone to think upon my sister's death. I need time to grieve in private for what I have lost," she said, hoping he would simply leave.

Pierce was not going to give up that easy. "But I would not be a true gentleman if I left you alone in such distress." He thought he had better move forward if his plan was going to work. "There is also more to tell you. Your brother is preparing to bring you back to England now that your sister is dead, but he has a problem. The situation has now changed. The war is officially ended and there are squabbles within The Holy Family and within the Brotherhood. Some have broken completely with the Duke. The Brotherhood here in America will no longer give him the same support as before, and is even beginning to splinter into different factions."

Mary was feeling frightened. All she wanted was to run away with Jupiter, but now, if she were to be caught up in political unrest, how would she ever escape? She knew she could not bear to lose her husband.

"I need you to know that my orders no longer come from the Duke, but from another here in America," said Pierce, taking a step forward which forced her take a step back. "I have been given instructions to ensure that you do not return to England. Any woman of The Vine is a treasure to be kept. And you, lovely Lady Mary, are a very precious treasure indeed." He moved forward again, and ran his hand down the side of her face. Again she stepped back, but now she was well inside of the cabin and Pierce was blocking the exit.

He grinned at her and said, "I knew when I first saw you that God had chosen me. I was chosen above other men because of my strength and courage. Do you know how much of this state I now own? Do you know how many slaves do my bidding? Do you know how many women would do anything to win my favor? Montford thought he was the one to enter into The Holy Family, but he is a weak and pathetic mouse—not a man. What would his seed bring to The Vine other than weak pathetic offspring? God favors the strong, and I am in God's favor!"

Pierce tried to grab her, but she ran further back into the cabin. He ran after her and knocked her onto the bed. Mary fought to get away, but only managed to knock the powdered wig off of his balding head before she was subdued. He had enough strength that he was able to pin both of her small arms with one of his.

"No! Not here! Not like this! This is not right without a proper marriage—and what of your wife," she said, desperately trying to get control of the situation.

Pierce just laughed. "Tragic things sometimes befall wives, and do not worry, my lovely Mary, a proper marriage will come soon enough. I am on a mission of God and I will not be stopped. Once my child is inside of you, you will be mine and I will take my rightful place within The Holy Family. Do not resist me woman. You will soon be glad that God has chosen me."

Pierce began to push up her petticoats. Mary tried to kick him while screaming at him to stop. In a desperate prayer she cried out, "Oh God, help me!" Then in the blink of an eye, Pierce was off of her and flying across the room. He crashed unto the table and one of the legs broke under his weight. It was then that Mary saw Jupiter standing near. He had heard her screams as he was returning from the woods.

"Are you hurt?" Jupiter anxiously asked.

Mary still crying replied, "Oh thank God, my love! Thank God you came back in time!"

Jupiter looked over at Pierce who was still on the floor leaning against the top of the broken table. Pierce had heard what Mary had said to Jupiter. His face twisted up in hateful anger as it all came clear to him. A slave had taken one of the greatest places of honour—a place that was rightfully his. Staring directly into Jupiter's eyes and grunting his words like an angry boar, Pierce said, "You are one dead blackie!"

With that, he sprang to his feet and ran outside in the direction of where his horse was tethered. Jupiter knew he would be going for a weapon and was right after him. Just as Pierce pulled a large hunting knife from his saddle, Jupiter swung him around and the knife flew from his hand. Without the knife, Pierce then tried to punch at Jupiter, but he was no match for Jupiter's strength. Jupiter pinned him with one arm up against the tree. The tethered horse whinnied in fear and moved away as far as it could. With his other hand, Jupiter grabbed Pierce by the throat and choked him. Pierce tried to kick, but Jupiter quickly pinned his legs against the tree with his own. The two men were locked together, face to face. Unable to move, Pierce could only stare—his bulging eyes full of dark evil hatred. Jupiter continued to crush the man's throat with every bit of strength he could muster. The grotesque rage in Pierce's face began to fade away, and was soon replaced entirely by the empty veil of death. Jupiter knew that it was done, and he released his grip. The lifeless body slid down the tree trunk, then dropped face first into the dirt and horse dung.

Mary ran up behind Jupiter and put her hands on his shoulders. She pressed her cheek against his back and wept loudly. He turned and took her in his arms and held her tightly. "We must take what we can and go now," he said. "They may soon come looking for him."

The sun was high in the sky as Jupiter tied their supplies to the horse's saddle. The original plan was to leave in the later evening in order to travel by the safety of darkness, but they could not risk the chance that someone may soon come looking for Pierce. Although it was unlikely that he would have told anyone about his trip to the cabin, they could not be certain. It was best if they simply got away as quickly as possible. Tomorrow they could return to traveling exclusively in the night.

Weeks before, Mary and Jupiter had decided that it was far too perilous to make their journey in the daylight. Mary knew that both the Brotherhood and her brother Charles had many eyes, and it was best to avoid being seen by anyone. Just in case they found themselves in a difficult situation, they had prepared a story about a war widow who was making her way north to her sister's home, but it was best if they never had to use it. The safest way was always to stay out of sight.

Jupiter finished tying the last bundle to the horse. He cut the rope with Pierce's knife and then put it into the sheath that was fastened to his belt. Turning to look at Mary he asked, "Are you ready?"

Mary smiled and placed her hand on his chest, "Yes, my love, I am ready."

Jupiter swung himself up into saddle then lifted Mary up and behind him. He pulled on the reigns directing the animal towards the river. From there, they would then head north.

Mary looked sadly at the little cabin as they passed it. She remembered how at first it looked only like a cursed hovel. Now, it was beautiful. It was place of refuge and salvation—a sacred place where she was awakened into the brilliant light of God's love. She wrapped her arms tighter around Jupiter's waist and rested her cheek upon his warm back. It didn't matter to her what was to come, only that they would stay together. Silently, she prayed,

Save us, O LORD our God, and gather us from among the heathen, to give thanks unto thy holy name, and to triumph in thy praise.

Chapter 22

As the two men rode up to the cabin, they could see no signs of life. Montford became immediately alarmed. He had been contacted by Pierce's wife who told him her husband had been missing for two weeks. It was not unusual for him to disappear for a few days without telling her, but he was never gone this long without sending word.

Before organizing any search for Pierce, Montford wanted to first confirm that Mary was safe. If Pierce had been attacked by Natives or a vengeful Tory, then Mary could also be in danger.

The two men dismounted, and tied their horses to the tree. Springsteen immediately noticed the remains of some old horse dung nearby, and knew that a horse had been tethered there sometime within the last two weeks. He looked around on the ground for more clues, but it had rained hard several days before so any prints had been washed away.

Montford rushed to the cabin, calling for Lady Mary. He was upset to find a pile of Mary's clothing spilled out on the bed, and the table broken on the floor. Springsteen came up behind him and said, "Well, something has gone awry." His eyes scoured the room for anything that could tell him more. "It was definitely not Indians," he added.

Montford rushed outside and looked in the barn and the shed. At first, he thought the cow was gone, until he noticed her several yards away grazing freely. There were also chickens left in the yard. He knew that whatever happened here was no simple robbery.

Springsteen, who had searched the cabin thoroughly, came out with Pierce's wig in hand and joined Montford in the yard. Montford looked down at the wig, but before he could say anything Springsteen asked, "Do you smell that?"

"Smell what? I don't smell anything," replied Montford.

Springsteen began to move in the direction of the odor and found himself in front of the woodpile. Montford followed him over and when close enough, he too noticed the horrible odor. Springsteen began to remove some of the logs. After removing several logs, a man's hand became visible. He moved a few more, and found himself staring into Pierce's decomposing face.

"Oh God," said Montford, covering his nose and mouth, and turning away. Despite the fact that he did not have the stomach to look at the ugliness of death, he was experiencing relief at seeing Pierce dead. Several days before, he had found out that Pierce was involved in secret talks with a high ranking member of the Brotherhood, and Montford had been worried about how to deal with the situation. Now this problem had been solved for him.

"Well, we certainly have found Brother Pierce," said Captain Springsteen, who felt no regret at finding his colleague dead, and was not afraid to show it.

"But where is Lady Mary?" said Montford, focusing back on the one thing that concerned him the most. "Do you think it was Tories? Could Tories have taken her?" he asked, even though he knew that no Tories were aware of her presence in America despite their own connection to the Duke.

After a thorough search of the area, the men found nothing that could help solve the mystery. Springsteen sat down on the stump near the shack, and tried to think about what may have happened. "Do you know why Pierce would be at the cabin when it was forbidden?" he asked Montford.

"I have no idea why he would come here," said Montford, looking into the distance. He did not share with Springsteen what he knew about Pierce's involvement in a conspiracy. Montford had to tread very carefully, and not divulge too much information. After all, he did not get this high up in rank by being foolishly unguarded. Some things should be kept to himself, especially since he was still unsure who had killed Pierce and why.

Springsteen suspected that Montford knew more than he was saying. Whatever happened to Lady Mary and Jupiter was likely related to the information Montford was hiding. There would be no point in investigating further. Springsteen had been in the Brotherhood long enough to know that it was often best to let sleeping dogs lie. With nothing else left to do, he decided that he must simply deal with the problem at hand, and focus on returning Pierce's body to his wife. The Captain then went into the cabin to find a sheet to wrap the dead.

Mary was surprised at how easy she was finding life on the run. She knew that she was not the strongest of women, and was worried that she would slow Jupiter down. Whenever she felt a little tired, one look at her husband helped her find the strength she needed. Being able to spend every day together, filled her with the hope that they would eventually find a sanctuary of their own. In the beginning, these thoughts alone were enough to make all of the discomforts of travel seem minor.

Jupiter knew all about surviving in the wilderness. Captain Springsteen had taught him early on how to find food, build shelters and even hide his trail. He was always quite at home in the woods, but this time he was filled with a new conviction. It was no longer just about survival—this time it was about living.

By riding at night and sleeping in the day, they were able to travel in safety and avoid being seen. However, early one morning just as they were setting up to camp for the day, someone happened to come across them. A woman from a nearby farm was out searching for a sheep that had wandered off. She had been drawn to their camp by the sound of the snorting horse. When she saw the couple, they were sitting on the ground in an obvious lovers' embrace. The woman screamed and ran off. At that point, Mary and Jupiter quickly gathered up their things and rode as fast as the horse would go. Once they believed that they were a safe enough distance away, they stopped to set up a new camp.

After that close call, Jupiter and Mary tried to stick to the heavily wooded areas as much as possible. For three more nights, they continued on horseback. At the end of the third night, they found a secluded glen that seemed a perfect place to set up camp. As they slept through the afternoon, their horse had somehow gotten loose, and ran away. From that point onward, they were forced to travel on foot.

Springsteen sat in a large armchair sipping brandy, and waiting to hear what Montford had to say. He had been called to meet Montford at his home, and was now concerned about what the man could want this time. He understood that the Brotherhood was going through some turmoil, and he had every intention of avoiding as much of it as he could.

Montford wanted to privately discuss with Springsteen not only the continuing crisis over the disappearance of Mary, but also the problem of the new divisions that seemed to be happening within the Brotherhood. The Duke of Compton had been double-crossed, and his power was now greatly diminished in America. Montford was no longer sure if he had any obligation to the man at all, and had not been in contact with him since the letter requesting the return of his sister.

Even if the Duke was no longer of any importance in America, Mary was still a woman of The Vine and he must try to find her. Montford was certain that, if she were still alive, she would not wish to return to England anyway. Surely, she had demonstrated such obvious affection towards him that she would want to remain in America. If he were to find and rescue her, then she would certainly become his wife, and he would be admitted into The Holy Family.

Montford nervously paced across the room, which greatly annoyed Springsteen. For him, there was nothing worse than a man who fretted like a woman. "For God's sake Samuel, have a large brandy," Springsteen said, rising from his chair and pouring a snifter full. He handed it to Montford.

Montford took the glass in hand and drank back a generous amount. The brandy immediately warmed him and helped calm his nerves. "I am unsure of my next move," he said, "and I need your advice."

Springsteen knew that what Montford really meant by 'advice' was that he needed him to do the difficult work that Montford was not capable of doing himself. It was not unusual for him to secretly ask Springsteen for help.

"I have been contacted by someone in The Highest Circle in regards to Lady Mary. I cannot say his name, but only that we need to take his requests very seriously. He has ordered that I not send her back to the Duke, but that I keep her here," said Montford nervously. He took another large swig of brandy. "I have not told him anything about her disappearance, but have merely sent word that I will do as he requests."

Springsteen had no patience for politics. He did not want to be a part of any deception and was annoyed that Montford had now involved him. "And have your scouts found no hint of where she may be?" asked Springsteen.

"There have been no signs at all. They have searched throughout the area west of here and have found nothing," said Montford. "I need your help to find her. You have friends among the Indians, and we can use that to our advantage. It is very important that, if she is still alive, we return her to safety. If we do not, who do you think will be blamed Robert?"

Springsteen knew if it came to that, he would likely take more of the blame than Montford. Long ago he learned that the lower your rung, the more you pay for the shortcomings of everyone above you. The Captain was just about to agree to help with the task when there was a knock on the parlor door.

"Come in," grunted Montford, as the brandy was now making him more irritable than relaxed.

A formally dressed house slave opened the door and ushered in a Patriot soldier whose uniform was well worn and very dirty. Springsteen could see from his tired looking face that he had gone through long periods of poor nutrition and too much whisky. In the Captain's experience, most of the foot soldiers had that look.

"I beg yar pardon, sir," he said, taking off his hat, "but I've some news that ya may wanna know." The hand holding his hat had three ugly stumps where his fingers used to be. "I was tellin' it ta some men in the tavern, and a feller in a fine coat said that I had ta come and tell ya all 'bout it."

"Well, what is it?" asked Montford, who was annoyed that this man was stinking up his parlor.

"A few days back I was north a' here. Up in Maryland—just a little north o' the border, when a woman, all upset, comes inta the inn where we was stayin'. Seems she come 'cross a blackie and a white woman in a field near her place." The man paused for a moment to gauge the reaction. He didn't want to tell too much more if it looked like he'd get into trouble. He knew that, for a man of his little education, it was easy to get into trouble without seeing trouble coming.

"What else did she say?" asked Montford anxiously.

"Well, she says that they was alone, and that they had a big black horse with them." The man paused again.

"Pierce's horse," Montford said aloud to himself. "Was the woman hurt? Did she scream for help? What else happened?" he asked frantically.

The soldier cleared his throat. More than once during the war he had been made to bear the irrational wrath of an angry officer, so he was a little hesitant to go on. "Well sir," he said, looking at the floor, "the lady that saw them was real upset. She said—she said the woman had her arms 'round the blackie's neck and was kissin' him on the mouth."

168

His words dropped like a ton of bricks upon Montford. "No, this can't be," he shouted, "The woman must have been seeing things. Does she drink? Is she known to lie?" he asked, desperate to find any evidence that the soldier's story was untrue.

"Sir, from what I know, she's a good respectable church-goin' woman. She don't drink and she ain't crazy. She was real upset by what she seen. Some o' the men went out ta the field and they found that somebody had bin there. But by that time, they was already gone," replied the soldier.

In shock and disbelief, Montford dropped his body into a nearby chair. How could this be true? He had spent hours with the woman, and had been so certain that she had been taken by his charms. She had said things that showed she was falling in love with him. This woman was his, and there was no possible way she could have chosen another—let alone a slave.

Montford suddenly remembered the intense passion with which Mary protested when Pierce was about to whip Jupiter. How could he have been so blind? He took another swig of brandy which fired his veins with anger.

Springsteen was surprised to find that the soldier's story made him want to laugh out loud. He stood up and turned towards the window where Montford and the soldier would not be able to see the smile he could no longer control. It was a mystery to him why he was finding the situation so delightfully amusing, but he was.

Montford looked at the soldier and realized that the man's worn dirty shoes were leaving mud on his carpet. "You can go now," he said with a wave of his hand. "However, you must talk no more about what happened in Maryland, or about our conversation here today. Rest assured that you shall be provided with compensation for your trouble. Just give your name and address to my slave as you leave."

The soldier was happy, for not only would he not to be punished for bringing what seemed to be bad news, but he would actually receive payment for his efforts. "Thank ya, sir," he said, then quickly exited the room.

After the house slave closed the parlor door behind him, Montford let loose. "Springsteen!" he shouted angrily. "This is your doing! You said that the woman would be safe with that slave! Surely she has been bewitched by magic. I have heard of African witchcraft being secretly practiced among them. Lady Mary would not have gone with him willingly. That black devil must have bewitched her!"

Springsteen could see that Montford was experiencing a severe blow to his ego at having been outdone by not just any man, but by a slave. On top of that, he was likely beginning to fear the eventual questions of those higher up. The Captain knew that in such a situation Montford would try and put the blame on him if he could. A man like Samuel Montford would sacrifice anyone to save himself, and Springsteen was damned if he was going to become some fool's sacrifice. He began to feel angry and frustrated with Montford.

"Jupiter knows no African magic," he said assertively. "If the woman went with him, she went because she wanted to. Needless to say, the Brotherhood will be asking questions, and we still must try to get her back. I will go to Maryland to the place where they were sighted. With any luck, I should be able to find their trail and catch up to them."

Montford was sitting with his head resting in his hand. The alcohol was now making him feel sick and dizzy. Without looking up, he said, "And when you find them Springsteen, be sure you return with only the woman. As for the blackie, do not even think about letting him live!"

Captain Springsteen did not respond, but merely turned and left the room.

Chapter 23

Mary felt weak and nauseas. She did not want to let Jupiter down, but she knew that she could not go much further without resting. "Jupiter, I am ill," she whispered in the dim light of the partial moon. She began feeling ill two days before, but said nothing about it. Now, she felt like the illness was taking hold worse than ever and she could no longer be silent.

Jupiter knew that it must be serious as Mary never complained about the hardships, even now that they traveled by foot. He took the small bundle she was carrying from her arms, and tucked it in with their other belongings and supplies that he carried on his back. "Let us go just a little further until we find a good place for you to rest," he said, knowing that they needed to find a more secluded spot for their safety.

In a short while, they came upon a sheltered place at the base of a cliff that had the remnants of a long ago campfire. Mary sat down, and leaned her body against the rock. The coolness of it brought her some comfort.

Jupiter dropped their bundles on the ground, and knelt down beside her. He put his hand to her forehead to check for fever. It was a relief to find that Mary's temperature was normal, but he was worried. What if she was really sick? How could he get help for her if she needed it? All he knew for sure was that, if anything should happen to Mary, he did not know how he could possibly go on.

"I should find some fresh water and wood for a fire. Will you be alright if I leave you alone for a short time?" he asked, not sure if he should go.

"Now that I am sitting down, I am fine," Mary assured him.

Jupiter placed Pierce's knife and the one full water canteen beside Mary. "I will leave these here with you, and will be back shortly," he said, and then disappeared into the darkness.

Mary began to feel ill again as she waited for Jupiter. It was not long before she heard the sound of someone approaching. Assuming it was Jupiter returning, she was about to say his name when she suddenly saw the shadowy outline of two men walking towards her. She tried to make herself as small as possible, and prayed that she would not to be noticed in the dim moonlight. Her fingers felt around for the knife that Jupiter had left, but she could not find it.

"Now what's this here?" said a voice. Mary was horrified to see two Patriot soldiers looking directly at her. She could see that their uniforms were in bad shape, and they looked as if they had been traveling for days.

"Why, it's a woman!" said one to the other. "What are you doin' out here?" he asked her.

Mary's head was spinning and her heart was racing. She was feeling even more nauseous, but now she had to try to concentrate on how she would deal with this dangerous situation. Running was certainly not an option, and her fingers frantically continued to search around for the knife that seemed to have disappeared completely.

"My name is Mary Powel, and I am a war widow. I am traveling from South Carolina to be with my sister in New York, but my horse is lost. I do have one slave with me who is presently searching for firewood. To add to my misfortune, I am also suffering from a mysterious illness, and had to rest here because I could go no further," said Mary, hoping that the men would simply take her story as the truth and move on.

"South Carolina eh?" said the one, who seemed to do all of the talking. "Well you sound like an English woman to me. You sure you're not English, and why are you travelin' in the dark instead o' in the day?" He leaned in a little closer, and Mary could see his leering unshaven face in the moonlight.

"Ah, come on now," said the other, speaking for the first time. "Leave her alone. The war's over, and I just wanna get home."

"You go on. I'll catch up," said the first soldier, waving his friend off, and keeping his eyes on Mary.

The second soldier simply shrugged his shoulders, and walked into the darkness leaving Mary alone with his companion.

Mary was still frantically searching for the knife, but still could not find it.

"What you looking for?" asked the soldier, as he moved close and quickly snatched up the knife that had been just out of reach of her hand. He squatted down beside her, and held the knife to her throat.

"Please," she pleaded, "I am very ill. Please leave me alone."

The soldier leaned closer into her, and Mary could smell a strong mix of whiskey and urine. "You don't look so sick to me. In fact for an English woman, you look kinda good," he hissed through his yellow teeth, as he ran his free hand down her arm.

Without warning, Jupiter suddenly rushed out of the trees. He held a thick wooden club in his hand.

The soldier flinched, but continued to hold the knife up to Mary's throat. "You just settle yourself down now blackie," he said. "I'm just makin' the acquaintance of your fine mistress here."

Mary remained calm and said, "You do not understand. I am very ill. Back home, the same illness killed six others in my family including my only child. I thought I had escaped its clutches, but now I have been struck down also. It is the angel of death, and if you do not leave now, you will certainly become severely ill."

"Yuss Sir," said Jupiter, hoping that he sounded convincing, "It killed most a' dem, and now it gots Missus

Powel here. Ya stay away from her now, if ya wanna live dat is."

Still pointing the knife at Mary, the soldier looked at Jupiter who smiled back at him in a simple-minded way. The soldier then looked back at Mary. It was true that the woman didn't look well, but she could be trying to trick him. He was certainly not going to be made a fool of by an English woman and a slave. "I don't believe you," he said angrily. "You're lyin' to me."

Mary could suddenly no longer control the natural urge of her body. In an instant she heaved and vomited all over the soldier.

"Oh mercy no!" shouted Jupiter. "Da angel of dead! It's on ya now! Dead! Dead! Dead! Yass gonna die masser! Yass gonna die fur sure now!"

The soldier, shocked and frightened by it all, dropped the knife and leapt to his feet. He began to tear off his soiled coat and breeches until he was almost naked wearing only his shoes and a dirty grey shirt. "Damned woman!" he shouted and ran off into the woods with his bare buttocks showing where his shirt-tail was missing.

Mary and Jupiter started to laugh. "You see my love," said Mary, now feeling much better. "I may be a small and weak woman, but I am not without my defenses."

Jupiter shook his head and smiled at her. "How do you feel?" he asked in concern.

"Actually," she said, "I feel much better. In fact, I feel well enough to do some more walking."

He helped her to her feet and asked, "Are you certain you can go on? I am worried about you."

"Yes, I am fine. We must keep moving just in case that soldier returns or tells someone else who comes looking for us." Mary picked up the water canteen, and washed out her mouth.

Jupiter began to gather up their things. "I suppose we can still travel a few miles before dawn."

Mary put her hand on his arm and said, "Then, my dear husband, we must take advantage of the darkness."

174

Chapter 24

As Captain Springsteen rode along under the cloudy sky, he hoped that it was not going to rain. Even a small amount of rain could possibly wash away the few signs that revealed the trail he followed. For the past week, the weather had been perfect for tracking, but now he began to wonder if both the weather and his luck may soon change.

Picking up Mary and Jupiter's trail had been easy enough. Once he was able to determine the location of the Maryland inn where the soldier stayed, it was a simple matter to find the woman who had come across the couple. When he found her, she was more than happy to tell Springsteen everything she saw, and take him to the exact spot where she had spied them.

From that point, the Captain was able to determine the direction in which they rode away, and then follow their path. They were definitely keeping clear of the main roads, and Jupiter was not leaving much evidence behind. A less skilled tracker would not have been able to pick up on the few and scattered clues, but Springsteen knew what to look for and how to find it.

As he followed their path into a little glen, he immediately noticed some indications of a campsite. Dismounting from his horse and tying it to a tree, he began to scour the area for more signs. He was surprised to see that the horse tracks had left the camp in a southerly direction. Upon closer inspection of the prints, he could see that the horse had gone alone and carried no rider. It was obvious to him that the beast must have either run away or Jupiter had purposely let it go. Without the telltale signs a horse leaves behind, this would make the trail more difficult to follow. However, it was also true that Mary and Jupiter would now be traveling at a much slower pace.

He continued to search the area, and uncovered an ornate black saddle that had been well hidden in the bushes. The double thunderbolts carved into the leather were unmistakable. This was the saddle that had belonged to James Pierce.

Examining the area even further, he was able to find some evidence that Mary and Jupiter were still headed north. This puzzled him. He could not understand why anyone trying to avoid capture would not eventually turn west and head into the deeper wilderness.

Springsteen's thoughts were interrupted by a deep growling sound, and he remembered that he had not yet eaten today. This was as good a place as any to stop and eat. He went to his saddle and removed a small bundle containing some dried fish and bread. Taking his canteen also, he then sat under a nearby tree to relax and enjoy his meal.

The Captain broke the bread in two, slipped the fish in the center and then sprinkled a little water over it. Leaning his back against the tree trunk, he took a bite then looked up at the grey sky as he chewed. Over the past few days of riding alone, there had been a lot of time to consider the strangeness of all that had happened. Previously, he had been so sure that he knew everything there was to know about Jupiter. There was no reason to doubt his slave's loyalty and obedience. It had never entered his thoughts even once that Jupiter would ever try to boldly escape, or that he would suddenly acquire a taste for women.

He tore into the bread with his teeth, and remembered the first time he had ever seen Jupiter. He had been intrigued by this well dressed boy being lead onto the auction block. Springsteen was a fairly young man at the time, and a new member of the Brotherhood. He had no intention to purchase a slave. It just happened that he was there with a fellow Brother who was looking to buy some laborers for his farm.

As Jupiter stood upon the stage, the room full of businessmen suddenly went quiet as though the boy had somehow commanded it. For what seemed like a long time, there was an amazing stillness in the air and no one uttered a sound. Then in an instant, the screech of the auctioneer shattered the calm, and the frenzied bidding began.

The rumor of Jupiter's father had already been strategically circulated prior to the beginning of the auction, in order to drive up the price. For many, there was prestige in owning a slave fathered by a man with such a high profile. Springsteen was not the kind to be swayed by this type of vanity, but he could not stop himself from bidding against those who were. There was something about the boy—something he could not explain that made Springsteen believe that Jupiter would be worth the inflated price. That day, he spent all of his money plus an extra hundred and forty pounds that he borrowed from the Brother.

Captain Springsteen swallowed the last of the bread and fish then took a long swig from his canteen. He stood up and returned to his horse. As he rode north, he thought about his current situation, and wondered at his own reaction to it. Initially he was thrilled to have leased Jupiter to the Brotherhood for such a large sum, but now for some reason, it no longer seemed important. Although he had received some payment up front, most if it he would never see. On top of this loss, there was also the loss of Jupiter himself. These financial setbacks would have, at one time, been very upsetting, but he found that it was no longer affecting him like it once would have. He was not the same as he was a few years ago or even a few months ago. The war had certainly helped to make him different. Having to kill so many and keep from being killed himself, had altered everything. What used to be so important to him before now seemed increasingly trivial. He was definitely a changed man, and it was only recently that he had started to be aware of these changes.

Springsteen saw some dark clouds far off in the western sky. Perhaps a heavy rain would come and wash away the trail. He then looked at the lighter grey clouds that were above his head. Their rain-free presence did not, however, fill him with reassurance. Instead, they only brought back memories of the deep blinding smoke of the battlefield. He remembered the many times the smoke was so thick, that he could not be sure who he was shooting at. All he could do was to pray that he was not killing his own men.

Springsteen thought about all the times he had cursed that damned smoke, and yet, there was one time when it cleared and he wished to God that it had remained. They had just fought a difficult battle, and the Patriots managed to get the upper hand. The British supporters who survived were forced to retreat into the woods. As the sound of the guns died off and the smoke faded, Springsteen scanned the field to assess the situation, and identify the positions of his men. A few of his men were dead, but it was mostly the British who were lying on the ground. He walked among his soldiers, congratulating them on a hard fought battle. As Captain Springsteen walked and shook the hands of the relieved and exhausted men, he found himself facing a soldier who would not look at him. The man's arms dangled at his sides and his musket was held loosely in one hand. He did not make any move at all, but just stared down at a dead Loyalist on the ground in front of him. Springsteen wondered if the man had gone mad during the battle. It happened more often than most would admit.

"Private!" Springsteen shouted, "Private, we won! You understand man? We won!"

The soldier turned his head and stared vacantly at his captain. Springsteen now wondered if perhaps he had gone deaf from cannon blasts, and again he shouted, "We won my man! It is time to celebrate!"

The soldier continued to stare at Springsteen in a strange and bewitched sort of way. Then suddenly his lips began to move, but nothing came out. The usually fearless Springsteen was suddenly filled with a feeling of sick-dread. The soldier dropped his eyes back down to the blood-soaked body at his feet and in a shaking voice that struggled from the depth of his throat he said, "That is my brother—my eldest brother Daniel."

Mary was feeling stronger and less nauseous. Her condition was definitely improving and she felt that the worst of her illness had passed. She was now able to keep valuable food in her stomach and to travel a little faster than before.

Their food supplies had mostly run out except for a small amount of dried fish. Mary did not realize that Jupiter now only pretended to eat his full portion of the rations. He was saving most of the remaining supplies for her.

Occasionally, Jupiter was able to scrounge up the odd bird or small rabbit, but years of war had helped to deplete the area of game, so it was not always easy to find meat. Even the edible wild roots and vegetables were harder to come by.

Jupiter had never traveled this far north in his life, and was unsure where they were, or what was ahead. Despite this, he never lost his faith. Regardless of the uncertainty of their situation, he had no question that they would find the safe place they dreamed of. Although he never lost hope, he worried a little about Mary and the strain of her illness. Sometimes her weakened body seemed to also weaken her spirits. Jupiter found that singing quietly to her often helped to restore some of her strength.

It was a sunny afternoon, and Jupiter and Mary lay asleep hidden in a little grotto that they had covered over with pine tree branches. They were both thoroughly exhausted from a long night of travel and were finding relief in deep slumber. Suddenly, the loud sound of a whinnying horse broke into their dreams. In an instant, they both opened their eyes and looked at each other in the dimness of their shelter. At first, neither was sure if what they heard was real, but then the horse cried out again and they held tightly to each other's hand. Jupiter reached behind him with his free hand and grabbed the knife that he kept nearby. He decided it was best if they stayed completely still and silent for the moment, and signaled this to Mary. It would be too risky to try to move some of the branches to look out as he could tell that the horse was very close by. The animal whinnied once again, and then they heard a man's voice say, "Whoa girl."

At the sound of that voice, Jupiter felt his heart nearly leap out of his chest, and a feverish heat ran through his body. Had they come this far just to have it all end here? For the first time in his life, he felt alive with hope and freedom. There was no way he would give it all up without a fight. He gripped the knife, ready to do anything needed to defend himself and his wife.

The man on horseback remained silent for what seemed like a very long time. Then suddenly he spoke again to his horse and said, "Time to go home Arcadia."

Mary and Jupiter listened to the sound of the trotting horse as it moved off into the distance and eventually could no longer be heard. Jupiter waited a moment until he was absolutely sure that there was no one outside of their shelter. He then slowly pushed away some of the branches and looked out. In the place where the horse had trampled down the plants and grasses was a small white bundle. Cautiously he climbed out of the hiding spot, still clenching the knife tightly in one hand.

Jupiter walked over to the bundle and squatted in front of it. It was a common enough looking package covered in a white napkin and wrapped up with string. He slowly and carefully untied the string and looked inside. "What is it Jupiter?" called Mary who was looking out from the grotto.

Jupiter smiled, showing his beautiful white teeth. "It is loaf of bread and some cheese," he said, holding it up for her to see.

Mary was confused. "Why would anyone drop bread and cheese out here, and then just ride away?" she asked.

"Anyone would not," said Jupiter, walking back towards Mary with the bundle of food in hand. "But apparently Captain Springsteen would."

Chapter 25

The farther north they headed, the more difficult it became for Jupiter and Mary to find suitable places to hide. The farms and towns were becoming more plentiful and the risk of becoming seen was more real. Still, they remained convinced that they should keep following the direction of Little Bear.

"Fair weather cometh out of the north," Mary would sometimes whisper to Jupiter to help strengthen their faith.

Early one morning, while the only light was still the moon, Mary and Jupiter came across what seemed to have been a once prosperous farm. From a small hilltop, they could see a large house and barn on the property, and although neither had fallen into complete disrepair, both buildings had certainly seen better days.

They slowly crept in closer and saw four large work horses in the barnyard. Past the barn, most of the fields were overgrown with weeds, but there was a large well-tended garden close to the house. The farm was not abandoned—someone still lived there.

For several days, Mary had been desperately craving the taste of milk again, and now wondered if there might be a cow in that barn. It was still early enough that no one would be awake. Perhaps it would be possible to sneak in, take a little milk and be gone without anyone knowing.

"Jupiter," she whispered, "could there be a cow in that barn?"

"I was thinking the same," replied Jupiter. "I can see no dogs to alarm the residents. Let me go first and I will signal you if it looks safe."

Mary did not like the idea of Jupiter going into possible danger alone, but knew that he was right. If someone did see him, he would have a better chance of escape on his own than if she were slowing him down. She waited quietly in the long grass and watched as Jupiter disappeared into the barn. Within a few moments, he leaned out of the door and beckoned to her.

Mary moved stealthily down the hill, and met Jupiter at the barn door. When they went inside, she was delighted to see three milking cows. Jupiter grabbed a nearby bucket and began to milk the closest one. Mary found a small dipper hanging on a nail. She scooped up the warm milk from the bucket then took a long slow sip. Nothing had ever tasted so good to her. She then handed the dipper to Jupiter who also drank.

After drinking all they could manage, they cautiously stepped outside the barn. The sun would soon rise, and it was beginning to rain softly. After traveling all night, the milk that filled their stomachs was making them more sleepy than usual. Many yards off, Jupiter spotted an old shed that sat a safe distance from the farmhouse. Weeds had grown up all around it, and it looked as though it had not been used in a very long time.

"We may have found our inn for the day," he said to Mary, who looked back at him and smiled.

They ran hand-in-hand through the light rain and towards the shed. Jupiter pulled hard to open the old door whose hinges had almost rusted shut. They went inside and were relieved to find that the roof was still able to keep the rain out. The shed was certainly dry and large enough for their comfort. Also, the solid wooden floor would make a pleasant change from sleeping on the cold ground. Except for a few old dusty household items neatly stacked in the corner, it was entirely empty. This was a perfect place for them to get some much needed sleep.

The rain was now coming down hard. It pounded loudly against the old roof which surprisingly did not allow the breach of a single drop. Mary was feeling safe and warm as she watched Jupiter spread out the blanket on the floor. Was this just a humble shed or, in reality, was it a beautiful castle? She joined Jupiter on the blanket, and they curled up with their arms around each other. *"My goodness, and my fortress; my high tower, and my deliverer,"* Mary whispered warmly against his cheek, and then they both fell into a very deep and peaceful sleep.

By midafternoon the rain had ended, and Jupiter and Mary were still sound-asleep in the shed. Suddenly, they were jolted awake by a loud horrible shrieking sound followed by a thunderous bang against the shed wall. Jupiter immediately sat up, and reached for the knife. Blinding light was streaming into the shed, and Mary and Jupiter quickly realized that the noise was from the old door being violently flung open. Jupiter pointed the knife, but at what, he did not know. His eyes were still trying to adjust to the sunlight that flooded into the shed. They could see only a single dark figure in the doorway, shadowed by the bright sun that shone behind. The figure stood there silently for what seemed like the longest time, and although Jupiter and Mary could not see the person, they could make out a musket pointing right at them.

The mystery person took a step forward, and was now completely in the shed. With the sun no longer directly behind him, he had come into the complete view. Although fairly tall, he was not much more than a boy with red hair and green eyes. His face was covered in freckles as plentiful as the stars that covered the night sky.

Jupiter was not sure what to do next. He still had the knife in his hand, but knew that it was no match for the loaded and ready-to-fire musket that was still pointed at them.

A large white smile with a bold gap between the two front teeth suddenly shot across the young man's face. In a voice that had yet to completely deepen, he chirped, "Ooow run'way blackies!" He then lowered the musket and put his fingers to his lips, indicating for Mary and Jupiter to be silent. "It's alright," he whispered. "I'z a blackie too."

+ + +

As Springsteen rode into Montford's yard, he couldn't help but feel a great deal of contentment. He had not intended to let Jupiter and Mary escape. His thoughts were to take Mary back and, unless he was forced to kill him, let Jupiter go free. Returning the woman would have made things much easier for him. He would have been a hero to Montford, who would certainly have rewarded him well. Now, Montford would likely try to punish him in small and covert ways for the failed mission. So why did the Captain feel so much satisfaction about what he had done?

Springsteen dismounted and handed the reigns to Montford's house slave who had come out to receive him. He had already thought about what he would say, and was well prepared to lie about ever finding them. With luck, Montford's more pressing concerns about divvying up the spoils of war and retaining power in the possibly fractured Brotherhood would make him too pre-occupied to worry about what had happened to the woman. Also, Springsteen was now certain that Montford would handle any enquiries by The Highest Circle with some fabricated story—a story that would likely not incriminate either of them.

The Captain did not go into the house right away, but instead paused on the porch. He looked at the blue sky and remembered the moment that he had come upon the tree bough sanctuary. The hiding place would have been invisible to most people, but Springsteen saw it right away and instinctively knew that Jupiter and Mary were still in there. It came as a surprise to him that, finally, after all the days spent tracking, he felt no satisfaction at finding them. For all the effort he put into following their trail, and even enjoying the hunt, he hesitated when it came to taking that final step.

For a time, he only sat on his horse and stared at those green branches. Jupiter had done a good job in camouflaging his hideout. It was Springsteen who taught him those secrets of surviving in the wilderness, and at that moment, he could not help but feel proud of his pupil's achievements.

As he continued to stare, a dark cloud that was covering the summer sun moved off, and the green of the pine boughs seemed to come alive in the bright light. Springsteen suddenly had a strange feeling. It was a feeling he remembered having only once before. It happened many years ago when he sat by his parlor window and was surprised to hear Jupiter singing in the yard. It had only been two months since he had purchased the shy boy, and Jupiter had barely said a word. But that afternoon, there he was singing the most beautiful song in the most beautiful voice that Springsteen had ever heard.

I will lie down in peace,
I will lie down in peace,
For you oh Lord, keep me safe in peace.

The memory came to him so clear and crisp, that it seemed as though he could hear young Jupiter singing that song from behind the branches. Without thinking twice about it, he quickly unfastened a bundle of bread and cheese that he had been carrying for his own supper, and dropped it to the ground. He then spoke aloud to his horse, calling her by name, in the hopes that this would somehow indicate his intention to never bother them again. It was then that Captain Robert Springsteen headed home.

"Captain Springsteen Sir, the Master is waiting for you."

The sound of the slave's voice jolted Springsteen back to Montford's front porch. He looked at the young man who waited with his eyes to the ground. This man had been several years with Montford, and Springsteen was suddenly aware that he knew nothing at all about him. "What is your name?" he asked.

"My name is Truth, Captain Springsteen Sir," he answered, with some obvious trepidation.

186

Springsteen clapped his hands and laughed in delight at the man's name. "Well Truth, I am delighted to make your acquaintance. How old are you?" he asked.

"I cannot say Captain Springsteen Sir, but Master Montford, he will know," replied Truth, still uncomfortable with Springsteen's interest in him.

"Well you are certainly old enough that you should have a wife by now," said Springsteen laughingly. "Everyman needs a wife to keep him honest. And if I am to be honest with you, Truth, then I must tell you that I do, in fact, have a wife of my own, and she has been my wife for a long time now."

Truth stood silently listening as Springsteen kept talking. "Montford does not know about her. In fact, now that I have told you, you and I are the only ones in this whole city who know. She is Cherokee and lives with her people. I have children too. There were four the last time I was there, and I expect that when I return, there will be a fifth. A wife and five children—can you believe that Truth—I have a wife and five children. Oh my friend, I must confess to you more. I must confess that I have hidden them away. Before—well—before things changed, I never admitted to myself that it was true—but yes, I can no longer deny what I have done. I have hidden them as if they were my shame, when truly they are my only hope." Springsteen fell silent for a moment and then asked, "Truth, do you ever dream of having a wife and children of your own?"

"I am a slave Captain Springsteen Sir, and slaves do not dream," Truth said, hoping this was a safe enough answer.

"You are a man," said Springsteen, "and every man has dreams." The Captain continued to stare at Truth, who continued to never look up at him. "Let me share with you one more secret," he said. "In this moment, I have decided that in the next few weeks I will be selling off everything I own, and then I will be on my way to join my family. I will never be returning here. If you like Truth, I will take you along with me. Not as a slave, but as a free man. It is a good place to live, and you can have the wife and children I know you must dream about."

For the first time Truth raised his head and looked directly into Springsteen's eyes.

"I assure you Truth that this is not a trick," said Springsteen sincerely. "In a few weeks, when I am ready to start my journey, I will come again to Montford's and see if you have made a decision. It would be a good thing if we could both find freedom. You need not say anything now, but just remember that when I go, I will take you with me if you like."

Truth smiled back at Springsteen, but said nothing. Instead he discreetly held out his hand and they silently shook on it.

✝ ✝ ✝

Mary and Jupiter looked at each other in confusion, and then back at the red-headed young man in front of them. Happily, he said to them, "I'z Henry. Don't be 'fraid o' me. I'z a slave too. Yuz stay here, and I'z git yuz somethin' fur to eat." Henry then stepped outside and closed the door.

Jupiter immediately jumped up, and checked to see if Henry had locked them in, but the door was even easier to open than before. He looked and saw the young man walking towards the house. He then quickly pulled the door shut again.

Mary looked at Jupiter and asked, "Is he to be believed or should we run?"

"He could have easily killed us if he wanted to do us harm. It is possible that he could be hoping for a reward for our capture, but if that was the case, he would certainly have secured the door from the outside. I believe that he is sincere," replied Jupiter. "I think we should trust him, at least for now."

"I also felt that he was sincere," said Mary, "and I agree that we should trust him unless he shows us the least reason not to."

Within the hour, there was a soft knock on the door of the shed. Jupiter opened it a crack and saw it was Henry balancing two plates of chicken stew in one hand, and a small bucket of clean water in the other. Jupiter opened the door wider to let him in.

Henry walked in and set down the bucket, and then handed one plate to Mary and one to Jupiter. "I had to sneak dese out de door so Mrs. Smit don't know and ask any questions," he said, turning and reaching over to close the door. It had been a long time since Jupiter and Mary had a proper hot meal, and they began to eat without delay. Henry laughed happily to see them enjoy the food he had prepared. "Yuz sure is hungry," he said, making himself comfortable by sitting cross-legged on the floor. Mary and Jupiter both sat down as well, but did not stop eating while they did so.

"So what yuz named?" asked Henry.

"My name is Mary, and this is my husband Jupiter," answered Mary between bites.

Jupiter had just finished scraping up the last of the food on his plate. He set it on the floor and extended his hand to Henry. "I am very happy to make your acquaintance Henry, and thank you so very much for the delicious meal you have provided us."

Henry shook Jupiter's hand and grinned. He liked Jupiter's fancy talk. "I'z de only one left now," he said, eager to have someone to talk to. "Me and Mrs. Smit is de only ones left. Mrs. Smit, her son David is my daddy. I'z look a lot like him, but David Smit left a long time ago. Got himself a wife, and headed west. My mama, she died a few years back, and now it's just me and Mrs. Smit. Mrs. Smit, she's too old, and can't take care a' de farm no more. It's sold to Mr. Stump, and tomorrow weez goin'. Everydin' is sold, and weez movin' up to New York. Dat's where Becky is. Becky is Mrs. Smit's girl. De wagon is packed up, and tomorrow weez goin'. Dat's why I come to dis old shed. Mrs. Smit told me to go look and see if dere was anyding here to take. When I seen de grass pushed down a little round de door, den I knew somebody might be here. So I got my musket. Sorry if I done scared yuz. Anyway, tomorrow weez goin' nord. Yuz goin' dat way too?"

"We are going north also," replied Jupiter.

"Maybe den I got a plan," grinned Henry. "Yuz don't wanna be slaves no more. I know all 'bout dat. I'z tired a' being a slave too. Soon it's my turn to run. But fur now, maybe I can help yuz?"

Mary and Jupiter smiled at each other. It felt good that Henry did not distinguish between them, and that they were both slaves in his eyes.

"If yuz like, we can all go in de wagon," said Henry, who was happy to have such excitement in his dull and lonely life. "Mrs. Smit, she's so old and mostly blind now. Can't see no ding. If yuz go in de wagon, yuz can ride as far as we go, but yuz mustn't make no noise. Mrs. Smit still hears real good. Anyway, it's a covered wagon so it's good fur hiding. But no sound—not even a sneeze. "

Jupiter looked at Mary, and then back at Henry's smiling happy face. He knew that they were at a greater risk of being caught now that they travelled through a more heavily populated area. If they were able to hide in a wagon, it would not only mean that they were less likely to be discovered, but it would also help them move faster. With Mary still not fully recovered from her illness, travelling by wagon would certainly make things easier for her. Jupiter decided that it was worth the risk.

"Thank you," he said. "It is very kind of you, and yes I believe that we will accept your offer to help us." He looked over at Mary to ensure that she was also in agreement.

"Yes Henry, thank you, and God bless you," she said.

Henry laughed. He was delighted to be a part of this exciting adventure, and the details of the plan had already been worked out in his head. He picked up the two empty plates and said, "Tonight, yuz stay here. Weez gonna leave early in de morning. I'z come get yuz when it's time to go. Will yuz do dat?"

"Yes Henry," said Mary, "we will wait for you to return."

Jupiter looked at Henry and nodded his agreement.

"Good," said Henry, opening the door to leave. "Tomorrow, weez all headed to New York." Without another word, he stepped outside and closed the door behind him.

That evening, as Jupiter and Mary lay together in the security of the old shed, Mary asked, "My love, are you worried that we still do not know where we are going?"

Jupiter ran his hand along her shoulder and down her arm. "Why should we worry? We follow Little Bear and Little Bear never lies," Jupiter softly laughed.

"With a whole world against us, are a few tiny stars so far away in the distant heavens enough?" Mary wondered aloud.

"Are you losing faith, my wife?" asked Jupiter, his voice full of concern.

"Oh no my love," replied Mary. "My faith may have faltered a little, but it is not lost. I suppose that I have still not fully recovered from my illness. Here, let me look upon your face and I will know that discomfort and misery are nothing but words."

Mary turned her head a little and in the twilight that slipped in past the slightly ajar door, she could see Jupiter's face. She placed her hand upon his cheek and said, "Before you, I was not truly alive. I appeared to others to live, but I was not living. Your kisses breathed life into me and when that happened, my eyes opened, my ears heard, and my hand touched for the first time. When you are near, it is impossible for me to lose my faith. Your hands are grace, your voice is salvation, your eyes are hope and your heartbeat is the love song of God."

Jupiter hugged her tightly. "I could not live without you," he whispered into her ear.

"Whatever happens, dear husband," said Mary, "whether we live or die, I shall not care. That we shall be together forever is all that I will ever wish for."

191

Chapter 26

The next day Mary and Jupiter awoke well before sunrise. They were feeling rested and eager to move on. After packing up their few belongings, they sat down close to each other and waited for Henry's arrival.

"Do you still feel certain that we can trust Henry?" asked Mary. The waiting was beginning to raise doubts and worries in her mind.

Jupiter took her hand and said, "Yes, I am certain that Henry is sincere. I cannot say why, but only that I am. I assume it is like the faith that keeps us following Little Bear. Faith tells me that Henry can be trusted, and at this moment I am very grateful that we have found a kind friend in such a scornful world."

Mary, feeling reassured, sighed and laid her head on his shoulder.

Just then, there was a quiet tap on the door. Jupiter peeked out, and when he saw Henry's smiling face, opened the door wide. "Well, dis is a good morning," said Henry, coming in and handing them another pail of clean water and two plates of breakfast. "Yuz ain't gonna be eatin' much agin til likely after dark, so better eat as much as yuz can now. I'z be back soon, den we all leave. Mrs. Smit wants to pull out nice an' early." Henry then hurried out of the shed, closing the door behind him.

Jupiter and Mary had barely enough time to eat and wash before Henry returned. He didn't say a word, but instead motioned for them to follow him. Jupiter put some leftover bread in his pocket, and he and Mary went out into the early morning light. Henry led them to a large and fully packed Conestoga wagon which was sitting near the house. They stood at the rear of the wagon, and watched as Henry climbed up then threw back an old blanket that was covering some items packed there. He gestured to Mary and Jupiter to climb up also. Jupiter helped Mary, and then climbed up after her. They could see that where Henry had lifted the blanket, there was a narrow tunnel formed by two large trunks on either side. An upside down table provided the tunnel with a roof.

"Crawl in dere," Henry quietly said, "Dere's a place in de middle fur hiding. Remember now, no sound, an' I'z call you out after we stop fur de night an' Mrs. Smit ain't around." He smiled happily at the thought of fooling Mrs. Smit. She was always kind to him, but only in the same way that she was kind to all of the animals that she owned. Never once had she ever acknowledged that Henry was her grandson.

Mary climbed over the back of the wagon and went in first. Jupiter followed, barely squeezing through the tight tunnel. Just as Henry had said, the tunnel led to a small open space encircled by Mrs. Smit's belongings. The roof of their little hideaway was a white sheet that was draped over the contents in the wagon. It softly glowed with the daylight that melted through it. Henry had provided them with several blankets, a few pillows and two canteens filled with water. The secret cave was small, and they could not stand, but there was enough room to be able to stretch out their legs and arms a little when they needed to move.

Jupiter unfolded one of the blankets and sat on it with his back against a wooden crate. He looked at Mary who had placed one of the pillows against the crate and sat beside him. He smiled at her, but said nothing. Henry had told them to always be quiet and he was prepared to do as Henry instructed. This young man was taking a great risk by helping them, and Jupiter was not going to do anything that could put them all in danger.

From outside, they heard a shrill old woman's voice calling for Henry. Henry, who was still at the back of the wagon, shouted, "I'z comin' Mrs. Smit! Just needs to load one more chair." Henry pushed a wooden chair into the tunnel space and dropped the blanket back over the load.

Jupiter and Mary sat crouched in their little sanctuary. Their faces glowed in the muted sunlight. Mary sighed and looked at Jupiter. She wished that she could tell Jupiter what she was feeling at that moment, but knew that it was best if they only spoke when absolutely necessary. They must respect the risk that Henry was taking on their behalf.

The little shelter was warm and the many wooden crates smelled of cedar. Mary leaned over and laid her head on Jupiter's shoulder. She thought about how not so long ago she walked through the most elaborate halls of England. She had kept company only with people who held great power and prestige. On many occasions, she had been a guest at the King's own table.

Now it was clear to her that it was all just foolish indulgence. No wonder there were so many days in England when she felt like she was suffocating—suffocating under the monstrous pile of the clothes, titles, expectations and lies. She walked among people who deemed themselves God's chosen, but what were they really? Mary knew that they were nothing more than tyrannical children performing a hideous play. It was only absurd theatre where every line, every gesture and every breath taken went nowhere and ended in nothing.

Mary ran her fingers along Jupiter's arm. He moved his arm around her shoulders and held her tightly against his chest. The loud strong drumming of his heart was something real and something true. *I am home*, she thought to herself. *I am home and I am alive*!

For five days, Jupiter and Mary traveled secretly in Mrs. Smit's wagon. They spent most of the daylight hours sleeping just as they had done before becoming stowaways. During the times they were awake, the necessary silence of their haven gave them both time to quietly reflect on all that had happened.

For Jupiter, there were no doubts in his mind that everything that had happened was for the best. He felt himself surrendering entirely to the natural way of freedom, and freedom was changing him. Just two months ago it would have been impossible for him to trust Henry, but he was no longer the same man he was two months ago. Jupiter knew he was different and was glad of it.

Occasionally, he was haunted by the memory of killing Pierce. He had never killed a man before, and found that there was nothing at all pleasant or satisfying about it. Now he would be forced to live with the ugly image of Pierce's dying face, perhaps for the rest of his life. Yet if he had to do it again, he would because it was necessary.

Jupiter knew for certain that there was nothing in his life more important than Mary. She had been the one who made him understand that he deserved better than what he was living. He fully realized that because she was a part of this Holy Family, they might never stop looking for her, but that was a risk he was willing to take. Mary was his life now, and he was confident that he was hers.

For Mary, the quiet times stowed away in the wagon gave her a chance to finally mourn her sister Ann. In the beginning, she blamed herself for everything that had happened, but she had come to recognize that none of it was her fault. She could not have saved Ann, and was now only barely able to save herself. Although she wished that things could have been different, she found solace in happy memories of her sister, and was determined to remember her in that light.

Mrs. Smit had planned her trip so that a day's ride took them as far as the next respectable roadside inn. She had decided that she was far too old to sleep under the stars anymore. Henry was not given a room, but was expected to sleep outside and guard the wagon against thieves. He always chose the most secluded area to park the wagon, and ensured that the rear was facing some woods or an empty field. That way Mary and Jupiter could get in and out without much risk of being seen.

Henry would knock three times on the side of the wagon to signal them when it was safe to come out, and he would always have a hearty meal waiting. He asked Mrs. Smit for extra portions, claiming that he needed more food to keep up his strength for traveling. He also dipped into some of the cheese, pickles and dried sausage that Mrs. Smit was taking in barrels to her daughter's home.

Before Henry went to sleep, he would enjoy sitting around the fire with Jupiter and Mary and listening to them tell stories of magic, mystery and strange creatures. He never asked them anything about their circumstances. It was likely the safest thing for everyone that he did not know too much—just in case. Henry merely relished the happiness found in the company of friends, even if it was only to be for a short time.

Early that morning, just before Mary and Jupiter scrambled back into their secret hiding place, Henry told them that they were getting close to the farm of Mrs. Smit's daughter. He estimated that they would arrive there the next evening before dark, and for that reason, they needed to be on their own way come nightfall. Mary and Jupiter were not bothered at having to continue traveling by foot, but they were unhappy that they might never see Henry again. He had certainly become their dear friend.

After it was dark enough, Henry sadly signaled to them for the last time that it was safe to emerge from their hiding place. He had greatly enjoyed the entire adventure, and having others to talk with proved to be a wonderful blessing. Besides his mother, Henry never had any friends before, and suddenly having the friendship of Jupiter and Mary helped him to see everything in a new light.

Henry sat by the fire and happily watched as the couple enjoyed the extra-large meal he had prepared. He could see the beautiful flames reflecting in their eyes and smiled to know that his eyes must look the same. For the first time in his life, he was feeling great pride. He alone had rescued these two people. He likely saved their very lives. Up until this point, he was only a mere slave boy to be ordered about. But now, he was no longer that boy or that slave. The day Henry opened that shed door and saw them huddled together on the floor, he immediately knew that, as an obedient and grateful slave, it was expected that he would either turn them in or shoot them right there. Yet in that moment, he chose to resist. In one bold move, he stepped out of his allotted place, and chose courage over servitude. Henry was just beginning to understand that, when he decided to rescue Jupiter and Mary, he had also opened a door for himself.

"I'z sure dat tomorrow we reach Becky's place," Henry said sadly. "I'm wishing I could take yuz furder along, but yuz can't be dere when de wagon gits unloaded. Tonight yuz best be gone."

Mary smiled at him and said, "Thank you dear brave Henry, for everything you have done."

"Yes," said Jupiter. "You have been very kind, and we will never forget how you have helped us. Thank you Henry."

Henry showed his big white grin and chirped, "I done fur yuz, just what I'z want somebody to do fur me. Being a slave, dat ain't a life fur nobody. Fur me, I'z taking Mrs. Smit to her Becky's and den I'z gone. I ain't no fool. I know I don't look like dey's 'specting slaves to look. I can go anywhere I want, where nobody knows me, and ain't nobody gonna guess. I got a little money saved up from some jobs I done. Dey say de west is a good place fur a young man to go git a start. So I'z goin' west."

"Well Henry, we wish you all the luck in the world," said Jupiter, who stood up and offered his hand.

Henry laughed merrily and shook hands with Jupiter. "Dat's good," said Henry, "cause all us slaves gonna need lots a' luck. We'd best all be wishing fur dat."

After Mary and Jupiter had finished eating, they knew that they should leave right away to put in as many miles as they could before daylight. Henry had provided them with three days' supply of cheese and sausage, and two canteens of water. He also gave them three of Mrs. Smit's best quilts.

They said their goodbyes, and Mary kissed Henry on his freckled cheek. In the firelight, they could see his face immediately flush red, and it made Jupiter and Mary laugh.

As the couple headed off northward into the woods, Henry called out a warning after them, "An' watch out fur Indians," he shouted. "Dey say de war left a bunch a' dem real mad, an' dey'll scalp yuz 'fore yuz can even blink!"

Chapter 27

Mary and Jupiter traveled onward for three nights. The rest they received while stowing away in the wagon had done them both a world of good. Mary had much of her strength back, and they were now able to cover a good a number of miles in that time. So far, fate was on their side as they had not been spotted by anyone except for one old farm dog who lazily looked at them, barked once and then walked away. Still unsure of where they would eventually arrive, they continued to keep the faith that north was the right way to go.

At the end of that third night of traveling, Mary and Jupiter came across what appeared to be a once prosperous estate. It had been burnt to the ground, undoubtedly at some time during the war. In the grey of dawn, they looked around at the devastation. What was left of the house and barn lay in two great heaps like piles of charred bones. The only things remaining intact were two tall stone chimneys that rose up in defiance out of the west and east sides of where the house once stood.

"This must have been a beautiful house," said Mary sadly. She imagined how it might have looked full of life and with fires burning in the hearths.

Jupiter put his arm around her. He couldn't help but feel the melancholy in the air, yet he was also thinking that this might be a good place to set up camp for the day. Behind the blackened heap that was once a barn, he spotted a small field stone building that was likely once used for storage. There were missing planks from the roof, and the door was nowhere to be seen, but the four stone walls were still standing strong.

He took Mary's hand and walked towards it. They could see that, to one side of the building, there was an old fenced-in garden now overtaken by wild plants. Jupiter hoped a few vegetables may have persevered and be hiding there. He would check through it later.

On the other side of the building were three young oak trees. The first was a red oak, the second a white and the third was a black oak. They had been planted in a neat row, and just far enough apart that their branches would be touching in a few more years. Mary thought how the people who had once lived here must have had such hopes that generations to come would enjoy the shade of these beautiful trees.

The couple peered through the doorway of the stone building. The sunlight that stole through the broken roof had caused a number of weeds to grow up from the dirt floor.

Jupiter looked at Mary, and could see that she was very tired. This made him suddenly become aware of his own exhaustion. "I believe that this should be a good place for us to sleep," he said, as he went inside the walls and began to pull up the weeds.

Mary leaned wearily against the stone wall. "It is perfect," she added.

After Jupiter had gathered some cedar boughs from nearby and placed them on the floor to make a bed, Mary unfurled one of the quilts that Henry had given them to cover them. She immediately toppled her tired body onto the makeshift mattress.

Jupiter left the hut, and walked over to some pine trees. He took out his knife, cut off several boughs, and then laid them across the broken roof to keep out the bright sun. He cut several larger branches to cover most of the open doorway.

After the branches were all in place, some sunlight did slip through the green needles, but it was dark enough for them to sleep. Jupiter curled up beside Mary, who was already fast asleep. He wrapped his arm around her, and listened happily to the sound of her breathing.

Although Jupiter was very tired, he could not fall asleep right away. Instead he found himself staring past Mary, and at the stone wall. He absently began to contemplate the technique that the craftsman had used to build it. It was certainly built by someone who knew what he was doing. As he studied how the stones were carefully fitted together, he suddenly became aware that among the many grey rocks, there was one that was different. A single white marble stone was tucked in close to the lower right corner, as if the craftsman deliberately tried to hide it. A moment ago, Jupiter did not see it at all. He had known nothing of its existence. It fascinated him to realize that having seen it, this one rock was now the only thing he could see. It was no longer a wall made of stones, but a wall that was built around that single white stone.

Any feelings of sadness he had felt upon first seeing the ruins of the farm were suddenly gone. Despite what violence and destruction had happened here, this was still a place of quiet peace and hope. Jupiter felt safe and secure in their little fortress. He pressed his lips to Mary's hair, and then closed his eyes and fell asleep.

It was early evening, and the sun had not yet set when Jupiter awoke. At first, he was disoriented and unsure where he was. Looking at the wall, he clearly saw the white marble stone, and only then remembered that they were camped at the burnt out farm. Jupiter smiled to himself. Sleep had not made the stone disappear back into the grey wall. Once seen, it was forever there.

He sat up and looked down at Mary, who was still asleep. He gently caressed her shoulder and whispered, "Mary, we must not linger here too long."

Mary had been dreaming that someone was after them, and they were trying to escape on horseback. The woods were dark, and the horses kept slowing down because of the thick underbrush. She knew that those in pursuit were quickly closing in, when suddenly she heard Jupiter's voice softly call through the darkness and her eyes opened. The sight of his face made the fear that had gripped her in sleep quickly melt away.

"I must go and see what I can find for our supper," said Jupiter. He stood up, stretched, and then moved to the door where he pushed away the pine boughs. Upon looking out, he made a dash back inside for the knife that was lying beside their bed.

Mary leapt up when she saw Jupiter frantically reaching for the knife. At first, she could not see what was outside as Jupiter was blocking the doorway. She moved a little closer, and looked out from behind his shoulder. There, she saw a Native warrior standing only a few yards away from the door. This was certainly more than enough of a concern, but then she looked to the right and left, and saw that there were at least seven warriors. It appeared that their small fortress was surrounded.

Jupiter stood ready to do whatever was needed. He had traveled with Captain Springsteen to many Native villages, and knew a great deal about the more southern tribes, but these men were different. Their dress, their faces and even their stance was not the same. Over the years he had heard many stories about the dreaded Iroquois, and was hoping that these were not them. It was clear that he was completely outnumbered, and at this point there was nothing he could do other than to wait for them to make the first move.

The warrior who was directly facing Jupiter suddenly turned, and in perfect English shouted, "Captain Pierpoint! We found them!"

Mary and Jupiter watched the warrior move to one side to reveal the striking figure walking towards them. He was a tall handsome African with a short well-trimmed beard, and was dressed in a very curious military uniform. Jupiter and Mary had never seen a uniform like this before. His coat was dark green and faced with crimson. Across his chest were two buff belts forming an 'X'. Where the belts crossed was a strange brass insignia holding them in place. The same brass insignia shone from the black leather cap on his head. His leggings were finely crafted from buckskin, and went from his waist to his ankles. On his feet, he wore moccasins.

As he walked towards them, Jupiter noticed that he did not walk like a slave, hunched over with apologetic steps, but instead stood tall, and sauntered proudly like any officer. The Captain stopped just a few feet away.

"Jupiter and Lady Mary, we have been searching for you," he said in a strange accent.

For a moment, they could not speak. This man knew who they were! Was he hired by Charles or by Montford? What was to happen to them now? Jupiter reached back and grabbed Mary's hand. If only they were not surrounded by so many, they could at least try to run.

Captain Pierpoint waited for a response, but there was only silence. "Do not be alarmed," he said reassuringly. "My name is Captain Richard Pierpoint. I was sent to find you, and to take you to a place of safety."

Jupiter was still unsure about the situation, but what were their choices? He turned his head and looked at Mary. Mary placed her hand on his shoulder and smiled. She then stepped past him and out of the shelter. She confidently addressed the Captain and said, "If you are truly our rescuer, then I thank God that you are here."

Captain Pierpoint removed his hat, bowed his head and said, "It is my privilege and honour to serve The Vine. Our camp is close by where we have horses for travel." The Captain then added, "We also have plenty of food, as I would assume that you must be hungry."

Jupiter smiled. He was now feeling certain that the Captain was trustworthy. First there was Henry, and now this man. Weeks ago, he had never imagined that there was even one person in the world who would want to help them, let alone two. "Yes," he said happily, "thank you, we are very hungry."

Chapter 28

Just as they had done in the beginning, Mary and Jupiter rode on a single horse along a riverbank. They felt secure knowing that Captain Pierpoint was taking them further north, and all through the calm and clear night, Little Bear pointed the way.

Eventually the stars disappeared with the rising sun, but the sense of peacefulness still remained. The only sounds were the songs of the morning birds, the bubbling of the river, and the rhythmic clip-clop of the horses' hooves.

Jupiter was not sure when he first became aware of the strange new noise. It seemed to come upon them so gradually. At some point he knew that he was hearing something, but was not sure what it could possibly be. It started out as audibly insignificant, but grew continually louder.

"Captain Pierpoint, what is that noise?" he called out to the Captain who rode ahead of them.

Captain Pierpoint seemed to laugh a little and shouted back, "That is Ne-ag-a, The Great Water Spirit."

Jupiter still did not understand. He looked at Mary who looked back at him and shrugged. Whatever this was, they were certainly moving closer to it as the roar became continually louder and louder.

When they finally came in sight of the great falls, they could not believe what they were seeing. Up ahead, the river they had been following suddenly dropped away and disappeared. As they moved closer, the gently sloping bank immediately changed to a steep foreboding cliff. The river had been sliced in two leaving one river above and one below. But between the two was a magnificent sight. In that great wound, the water was transformed into a wall of glowing white cloud. At the bottom of this wall, much of the white cloud refused to return once more to water, and instead leapt upwards, and disappeared into the air. This was a sacred place—a place where the sky and the earth were one. 'I Am Living Force' it roared without pause, as the gentle spray sprinkled over Jupiter and Mary.

They all stopped their horses for a moment to get a good look at the beautiful sight. Then Mary saw something in the distance that she could hardly believe. She pointed it out to Jupiter. Farther up the wide river and to the right of the falls was yet another even larger waterfall. There were two—two places where the earth and sky were united as one.

Mary whispered in Jupiter's ear. "Can you believe it? It is real my love. Do you remember the stories? The stories you and Simon told to one another. Remember what you told me about the river creature that roared so loud to guard the secret land. It is true Jupiter! Your dream has become real!"

Jupiter stared into the glowing white water and began to surrender completely to its mist. Soft cool moisture gathered on his face and in his hair. It slowly began to roll in small droplets down his skin. At this moment, he remembered something he had read in the Bible. They were words that had stayed in his mind—words that waited for a place and a time—words that had waited for now. No one could hear him over the roar of the falls as he quietly whispered into the moist air,

Yet through the scent of water it will bud, and bring forth boughs like a plant.

205

As they entered Fort Niagara, Mary and Jupiter were immediately struck by the impressive stone fortress that looked as if it had just risen up from the rocky shoreline of the lake. Surrounding this building were many smaller temporary shelters including several longhouses. There were a great number of people of all sorts. Men and woman who had been going about their business stopped to watch as the party the rode in. Children seemed to be everywhere. The ones old enough to be out of a mothers' sight designated themselves official escorts for the newcomers, and began to follow alongside the horses.

The party dismounted outside of the main entrance to the stone building. Captain Pierpoint led Jupiter and Mary inside, and then ushered them into a room where a fully uniformed British officer rose from behind his desk to greet them. "Lady Mary and Jupiter, I am so glad that Captain Pierpoint has found you," he said, bowing like a gentleman. "My name is Colonel Betts, and I would like to welcome you to Fort Niagara."

Mary smiled and said, "Thank you Colonel Betts. We are grateful for your kindness."

Jupiter extended his hand towards the Colonel who happily shook it. "Yes, we are both very grateful," he added.

Captain Pierpoint, eager to return to his family, interrupted and said, "I do not wish to be rude, but I am afraid I have urgent matters to attend to in Grand River. Therefore I must excuse myself."

Colonel Betts stepped out from behind his desk and warmly clasped the Captain by the arm. "Thank you Richard. As usual, you have done us all a great service."

The Captain silently bowed farewell to Mary and Jupiter, then left the room.

"That man," said Colonel Betts, "is one of the bravest and most intelligent men I have ever known. The Crown owes him a great debt of gratitude, but I fear they will never properly repay what they truly owe." The Colonel then pointed to two leather chairs in front of his desk. "Please," he said, "please sit. You must be very tired."

Mary and Jupiter melted into the soft chairs which, after enduring weeks of discomfort, felt immeasurably luxurious. Still, they could not fully relax. There were many questions going through both of their minds. Jupiter spoke first and asked, "Colonel, how do you know us, and why do you welcome us here?"

Colonel Betts walked over and sat down behind his desk. "We were told of you by The Duke of Compton, who ordered that we keep our eyes and ears open for any sign of where you might be."

Mary sprang from her chair. She looked over at Jupiter in panic. How could she have been so foolish as to trust this man who wore the British uniform? She wanted to grab Jupiter and run, but where would they go? Her eyes flashed at the sight of the open door, and she reached for Jupiter's hand to take him with her.

"No, you misunderstand!" cried the Colonel, deeply concerned that he had not chosen his words more carefully. "I have no intention of handing you over to your brother."

Mary looked into the eyes of Colonel Betts, unsure if he were lying. He smiled at her, and hoped that she would see that he was genuine. Jupiter gently pulled her back, and she sank into the chair again. The fright had been too much to bear, and she immediately broke down and wept into her hands. Jupiter leaned over, and gently caressed her shoulders.

"I am so sorry that I alarmed you, My Lady," said the Colonel apologetically. "I assure you both that you are safe here, and that the Duke will certainly not be informed of your whereabouts."

Jupiter looked at Colonel Betts. "We are very grateful for your kindness, but why do you want to help us?" he asked, curious about the Colonel's motives.

Colonel Betts said nothing at first. He merely got up from his chair and walked over to the window. For a while, he just stood there and looked out, until finally he turned back to the couple and replied, "What do I owe the Duke? What did he do to stop this war from happening, and once it happened, what did he do to end it? I have lost so much—my home, many friends, but most of all, my only son. At one point, I almost lost my wife and daughters as well. I have killed old neighbors, and have had old neighbors try to kill me. All that I could, I gave to the British cause, and for what? So the stroke of pen could turn sacrifice into just a meaningless word. Now, we have even been given instructions that we must hand over our own sweet Fort Niagara, for which we fought so hard. No, I owe nothing to the Duke."

Colonel Betts walked back to his chair and sat down. "If this war has taught me anything, it has taught me that my oath to the Brotherhood and even to The King means nothing in the face of my oath to God. As long as you need a place to live safely Lady Mary and Jupiter, I will help provide this. Not only is this my desire, but it is also my sacred duty as a Christian."

Mary sighed in relief. Had they really found their sanctuary? She looked questioningly at Jupiter who smiled with confidence and said, "Well, my wife, it looks as though Little Bear has taken us home."

She leaned over, kissed his cheek, and then turned and smiled at Colonel Betts. With deepest sincerity, she said,

I was hungry, and ye gave me meat; I was thirsty, and ye gave me drink; I was a stranger, and ye took me in.

Colonel Betts felt his eyes begin to water. It had been a long time since his war-ravaged heart had been able to feel much of anything other than anger and frustration. Throughout the conflict his faith had dwindled away, but now the light was starting to shine again. Looking at Jupiter and Mary sitting before him, Colonel Betts silently said a prayer of gratitude for all that he was now feeling, *hope deferred maketh the heart sick: but when the desire cometh, it is a tree of life.*

Chapter 29

Mary sat at the table peeling apples for a pie she was preparing for their supper. She paused and looked out of the nearby window. Many of the trees had begun to change color, and the midday sun now hung low in the sky. Winter was not far off.

Five years had passed since they made their way to safety, and three years since they had moved across the river to Butlersburg. As Fort Niagara would eventually be handed over to the Americans, many refugees had followed Colonel Betts here, with the hope of finally living in peace and safety.

Mary looked around at the tidy little cottage. She loved her modest cedar plank house with its single all-purpose room on the ground level and two bedrooms in the attic. Its humbleness reminded her so much of the cabin that was her first real home with Jupiter.

She looked down again at the apple and knife in her hand. Carefully she sliced through the red skin and revealed the hidden white fruit beneath. The juice covered her fingers and irritated a small cut she had on her thumb. This pain made her suddenly recall an incident from her childhood. When she was very young and just learning needle point, she had somehow accidentally shoved the needle into the palm of her hand. At first, she did not feel anything, but the sight of the needle filled her with terror. For the longest time, she was too fearful to even move. In her child's mind, it seemed like the needle was in so deep that it could never possibly be pulled out. She felt forever pinned in place, like a mounted butterfly. Eventually her nurse noticed her, and quickly pulled the needle from her hand. Only then did she feel the pain and begin to cry.

Before Jupiter, that had been her world. She had been as if dead—unable to move, or to speak, or to fully feel. It was only through the grace and mercy of love that the needle could be removed. Only then could she come to life. Mary began to peel another apple and thought, *God gives water not gold to the chosen.*

The door suddenly opened, awakening Mary from her deep thoughts. She looked up and smiled with pleasure to see Jupiter smiling back at her. He closed the door, and sauntered into the room. Without a word he kissed her on the cheek, and then sank down into a stuffed chair that sat beside the glowing fireplace.

Mary knew right away that something was on his mind, and that it was something that he knew she would not like. She continued to peel the apples, and waited for him to get up the nerve to tell her what it was.

"This evening I am going hunting with Kwa-yo. He has asked me many times before, and I promised him that, tonight, I would go," Jupiter said quickly.

Mary wiped her hands on her apron, then went over and sat on Jupiter's lap. She wrapped her arms around his neck and said, "You know that I am concerned when you are out in the evening. Would you not rather just stay home?"

Mary understood that Jupiter needed to live as freely as any man, but she could not help but worry. She wished that she would always be able to keep him safe. However, she knew that she could not even guarantee that for herself.

"Mary, do not fret," said Jupiter, running the fingers of his left hand back and forth along the nape of her neck. "I will be fine. There will be more than just Kwa-yo. Two others will be joining us. They are all skilled hunters who came through the war without a single wound. They would recognize any danger before it was upon us."

Mary looked into his eyes and said, "I know that I should not worry my husband, but I could not live if anything was to happen to you."

Jupiter put his mouth to her ear and whispered, "I have already promised that we shall never be parted, and I am a man of my word."

Mary turned her face towards his and kissed him passionately.

Suddenly, the door flew open and crashed loudly into the wall. Mary and Jupiter both jumped up together. Rebecca, a Seneca woman who worked for Colonel Betts, was standing in the doorway. Before Rebecca could even say a word, Mary knew that she and Jupiter needed to leave immediately. From the beginning, the Colonel promised that he would provide them with a warning and means of escape if such a time came. They accepted and lived with the possibility that one day the Duke may learn where Mary was hiding.

"The horses are here! Go now!" Rebecca quickly said.

Mary and Jupiter ran out of the cabin where they found a young boy holding the reigns of two horses saddled and waiting. They quickly mounted them and galloped towards the road which ran south along the river. Somewhere behind them they could hear a distant voice shout, "Halt!" but they did not dare waste any time by looking back.

Colonel Betts was busy sorting out a seemingly endless pile of paperwork. He was beginning to feel that bureaucracy was proving a more formidable enemy than any Rebel. When he heard a knock at the front door, he did not think much about it. There were always settlers with problems, and it was normal for his day to be full of interruptions.

He was surprised when Rebecca showed up at the office door with a fully uniformed British General. The General was easily recognizable as a man of great importance, and was surprisingly young considering his rank. His coat was the richest shade of red, and his immaculately white breeches and stockings were of the finest cloth. He stood taller than your average man, and had a handsome face. When he spoke, he spoke with the accent of England's highest society.

"Good day Colonel Betts," he said, without offering a handshake. "I am Lord General William Phillippe, cousin to The Duke of Compton."

The Colonel knew all about William; first from his connection to the Brotherhood, and second because Mary had filled him in on the complete story. He smiled politely trying not to show the alarm he was feeling. Turning to Rebecca, he quickly said, "We are honoured to have a very special guest. Prepare our finest tea."

Rebecca looked at the Colonel knowingly, and then hurried out.

"I am afraid I have no time for tea Colonel," said William. "The Duke has heard that his sister may be hiding here at Butlersburg, and has requested that I personally come to find her."

"Here?" said the Colonel, trying to sound surprised. "We have many refugees within and around the town, but certainly not such a woman as an English lady of noble birth. Are you certain of your information?"

William looked into the Colonel's eyes, and tried to decide if he knew more than he was telling. "Colonel, I need not tell you that she is suspected of being in the company of a Negro. You received that information years ago when you were still at Fort Niagara. At that time, you were ordered to inform us, without delay, if you should ever hear of her whereabouts. Are there any at all here in Butlersburg that would even vaguely match the description of these two?"

Colonel Betts answered honestly and simply replied, "There are several families of that or a similar description in and around the town, but none of those women are the sort who would be found in any English courts."

William was beginning to feel annoyed with Colonel Betts. He already deeply resented being sent on a mission that required him to leave the comforts of England, and now he was feeling even angrier that this colonist may be trying to deceive him. He looked down at the buckskin leggings the Colonel was wearing, and sneered. It suddenly became obvious that Betts was of an even more inferior breed than most British American officers. The man could not possibly be capable of any level of sophisticated deception. He was clearly simple-minded, and without the ability to grasp the serious situation at hand. Such men fight well during war, but have little use in times of peace.

Deciding it was best if he were to just take charge and move fast, William said, "I have four men waiting outside, and we shall be thoroughly searching the area for my cousin." He then turned towards the door.

"Wait," said the Colonel, trying to stall a little longer, "would you not like some tea first, Lord General, or perhaps a glass of brandy?"

"No," he replied. "There is no time to waste. I need to return to England as soon as possible, and I intend to take my cousin Mary along with me."

William then marched out of the room and headed towards the front door. Colonel Betts was right behind him hoping that Rebecca had been given enough time to warn Jupiter and Mary. He was trying to think of something else to say that would delay the search.

As William brusquely walked out to his men, who were waiting with the horses ready to go, he glanced towards the river and saw in the distance two horses carrying a man and a woman galloping at a high speed along the road. As loud as he could he shouted "Halt!"

Mary was certain she recognized her cousin's voice, and knew that she and Jupiter had to run for their lives. They urged their horses on as fast as they could go. Unfortunately, the only horses Rebecca could find quickly were a couple of older mares. Mary hoped that they had enough of a lead to outrun William and his men.

They continued to gallop south along the road that ran parallel to the river. Once they passed the falls they could turn their horses west, and head into the dense bush. From there they could make their way to Grand River.

The hooves of their horses pounded into the ground and for a long time it seemed that their escape plan was working. As the roar of Ne-ag-a grew closer, they knew that they were also closer to reaching safety.

The beautiful falls finally came into view, and they rode through its cool mists. Just a little further and they would reach the hidden trail that would deliver them far from harm.

Without warning, Jupiter's horse began to slow. Something was wrong. Mary slowed hers down also. Suddenly, Jupiter's horse dropped to the ground. Mary pulled on the reigns and turned around. She saw Jupiter standing next to the fallen mare whose eyes bulged in impending death. There was blood flowing from her white flank, and it was clear that she had been shot.

Mary shouted, "Get on my horse!" But before either of them could make a move Mary's horse was also shot and collapsing underneath her. She jumped off and grabbed Jupiter's hand, but there was now nowhere to run. William and his men had quickly ridden in, and were to the front and sides of them. For a moment, the couple stood frozen, but then slowly they backed up into the wildflowers and grasses that grew along the riverbank. They were trapped with the armed men in the front and the river behind.

William was pleased that the discomforts of his journey to America would prove to be worth it after all. Instead of moving in right away, he wanted to savor his victory and remained on his horse where he just stared triumphantly at Mary. He chuckled to himself at her dowdy dress. Perhaps he should save the costume to embarrass her back in England. It would get a fine laugh at parties.

Mary listened to the thundering water. She looked over at Jupiter, who looked at her and smiled. She knowingly smiled back. Then they both dropped to their knees facing each other. The noise from the falls meant that only Mary could hear Jupiter when he said, "My dearest wife, we were born so far apart that only the miraculous power of Grace could bring us together. And when we became one, something wonderful happened. Our gift was a gift, not just for two, but for all men, women and children. Our treasure was God's treasure on earth. As we now kneel before God, we know what would happen if the wicked should ever lay their hands on us."

Mary looked at her husband and sighed, "My love, I wish it could be different, but you are right. How many times have you promised me that we would be together always? You know that you are a prophet." Mary then put her hands together and staring into Jupiter's eyes she prayed,

Our Father and Mother who art in Heaven
Hallowed be thy name
Thy Kingdom come
Thy Will be done
On earth as it is in Heaven

As William watched the two pray, he smiled gleefully. Not being able to hear what Mary was saying, he merely assumed that they were begging him for their lives. It made him giddy to see her on her knees in the mud. He wondered if he should shoot the Negro now or later. He then decided that it was best to drag out this sweet moment as long as he could. At this point, William was content to simply watch his cornered prey squirm.

Mary and Jupiter, still facing each other, stood up, and then fell into a passionate kiss. William's grin dropped in sudden fury. How dare this woman flaunt her unnatural desires in front of him! That she would reject him as a husband, and then cling to this inferior creature was bad enough. If she had any sense, she would now be begging for forgiveness not defying him further. It was then that William decided he would make her watch the Negro suffer before he killed him.

Just as he signaled to his men to seize them, the pair suddenly disappeared before his eyes. "What?" he shouted, unable to believe what he had just seen. He jumped down from his horse, and rushed forward to the place where they had been standing. There, he found himself right at the water's edge. He looked down the river, and saw Jupiter and Mary being quickly carried away in the northbound current. Despite the power of the water, they never let go of each other. The river then delivered them straight to the precipice, and in an instant they disappeared together into the pure white rising mist of Ne-ag-a.

Chapter 30

Colonel Betts was at first delighted when he saw William ride back into Butlersburg with neither Mary nor Jupiter. He thought that this surely meant they had escaped. The look of failure on the Lord General's face as he dismounted was a very welcome sight.

William stared angrily at the Colonel for a moment, and then without a word stepped past him and into the house. The Colonel was annoyed that this man would just walk uninvited into his home, but knew it was best if he just quietly followed behind. William marched straight into the Colonel's office leaving a trail with his mud covered boots. He unceremoniously plopped down on one of the stuffed chairs.

"I almost had them!" he said to the Colonel. "I was so close, and should have taken them when I had the chance. I could never have imagined such a thing. I knew the woman was mad, but to jump with that Negro into the river? This, I never expected."

Colonel Betts felt his heart sink. More than anything he wanted to grab William by the throat and send his dirty soul straight to Hell were it belonged. He knew, however, that this would jeopardize everything. Instead he turned his back to the man, and began to pour out two glasses of brandy. During the war, he had discovered his hidden personal strengths, and those same strengths must now sustain him through this impossible situation. Letting his feelings show, even a little, could be catastrophic. A great treasure was at stake, and he was bound to protect it at all costs. With his back still towards William, he asked, "Would you like the brandy now?"

"Certainly I will take it now. Give it here Colonel," said William, eager to calm his shattered nerves. "Even colonial brandy would taste good at this point."

The Colonel turned, and handed him a large full glass. As William reached out his hand, Colonel Betts noticed that it was shaking. He thought to himself, *the wicked tremble and fear before the Living God.*

"The Duke will not be pleased," said Lord William, taking a huge gulp that almost choked him. "With all that has happened within the Brotherhood, and now this! He will certainly not be pleased."

Colonel Betts did not respond, but only watched as William drank back some more whiskey, and then grunted, "I cannot believe that she would do such a thing! What was wrong with that woman? What possessed her to behave so? She chose death over returning to England?" William shook his head in disbelief and went quiet.

For a while, the two men just remained in the thick silence sipping back the whiskey, and staring at their glasses.

Suddenly without warning, the silence was shattered when life and laughter burst unceremoniously into the room. It alarmed the already frazzled William, who immediately placed a hand on his sword, but then relaxed in annoyance when he saw it was only two little girls who had run playfully into the office. They were very young and appeared to be around the ages of two and four. The pair laughingly ducked behind Colonel Betts' desk.

William was disgusted by this intrusion. Everything about Upper Canada disgusted him. He gulped down the last of the whiskey, and then quickly stood up. "I have had my fill of this place," he declared angrily. "The sooner I am out of this savage and foul land the better."

The Colonel looked down nervously at the girls, who were peeking out from behind the desk. William looked at

Colonel Betts, and then at the girls. He laughed wickedly and asked, "Are those your mongrels Colonel?"

Colonel Betts held his anger, smiled politely and said, "No Lord General, they are the daughters of my housekeeper Rebecca."

"And you are sure then, that they are not yours?" asked William, fishing for any gossip he could take back with him to England.

"No Lord General," replied the Colonel. "Rebecca has a husband and I am not him." He was relieved that all darker skinned people looked the same to William.

"Well then," said William, disappointed but prepared to spread the tale anyway, "I shall be on my way. The sooner I return to England the better."

"Whatever you feel is best Lord General," said the Colonel, glad that the man would not be staying around Butlersburg.

William then placed his empty glass on the desk, and without a farewell or a thank you, he marched out the door.

Colonel Betts was relieved that William was now gone. He set down his mostly full glass and slumped into the chair behind his desk. In his mind he could see Jupiter and Mary as if they were still there, but he knew it was not true. They had made their final escape. The tears he had held back before began to well up in his eyes.

The two little girls now standing to the side of his chair looked at him curiously. The older one reached over and patted his arm. "There, there Uncle John, it will be all right," she said.

The littler one said nothing, but like her sister reached over to pat his arm. He looked down at their lovely brown faces, and couldn't help but smile. The girls smiled back, and first one then the other scrambled up into his lap. They both began to shuffle through the papers on his desk. The older girl picked out words she recognized, and read them aloud to her sister.

Rebecca came into the room. "He is gone?" she asked, and waited for the Colonel to say something she wanted to hear.

"Yes Rebecca, he is gone," said the Colonel, trying to decide how to tell her the bad news. Choosing his words carefully he added, "Rebecca, you know that they were prepared to do anything not to be captured. They knew what it could mean if the Duke were to find out about the treasure."

The Colonel did not have to say anymore. Rebecca knew what he meant. She put her hands to her face and began to sob openly. Quickly, she left to find others who could mourn with her.

The two little girls silently watched Rebecca leave. They were surprised by her tears, and the seriousness of the exchange, but were still too young to really understand such sadness. The intense world of adults was something they had not yet discovered, and for now, only glimpsed with mild interest from afar. Shortly after Rebecca left, they went back to playing with the papers.

The Colonel sighed and marveled at their happy innocent play. He wondered what he should tell them. It would not take long before they realized that their parents were gone. Regardless of what they would eventually be told, he knew that it was his duty to protect these treasures with his very life. He softly placed both of his hands on the top of each girl's head. He ran his fingers back and forth across the crown of their skulls. It was unmistakable even through their soft, thick curls.

"Glory be to God," he whispered softly, "Two Holy Grails."

www.ingramcontent.com/pod-product-compliance
Lightning Source LLC
Chambersburg PA
CBHW070019120726
47909CB00003B/997